TALES FROM THE ARABIAN NIGHTS

Tales from the Arabian Nights

Translated by
Vera Gissing

Edited by
Anne Scott

Illustrated by
Mária Želibská

GALLEY PRESS

First published 1981 by
Cathay Books Limited
59 Grosvenor Street
London W1
Retold by Vladimír Hulpach
Translated by Vera Gissing
Graphic design by Jiří Schmidt
This edition © Artia 1981

ISBN 0 86178 055 8
Printed in Czechoslovakia by PZ Bratislava
1/18/04/51-01

A THOUSAND AND ONE NIGHTS

Many centuries have passed since the days when in a distant Arabian land the beautiful Scheherazade related her wondrous tales to the caliph Schahria. Some tales are humorous, others touching; some filled with kindness, others with cruelty. They tell of historical characters, such as Haroun al Raschid, the former caliph of Baghdad, and of other figures, whose names became familiar only in later years, like Ali Baba and the forty thieves, and Aladdin and the magic lamp. The stories bring to life good and evil spirits, genies, snake queens, witches and wizards. But the ordinary folk always have the last word, whether they are from Baghdad, Cairo, Basra, or the country; whether they are potters, goldsmiths, dyers, cobblers, blacksmiths or bakers. A tremendously wide variety of human character is assembled here. You will find people who are kind and honest and easily pleased, as well as those whose hearts are filled with envy and greed, tricksters and swindlers.

The stories reflect the true temperament of the Arabic people and a way of life so different from ours; now and then they are affected by the historical conditions, in which the co-existence of three different religions has played a most important part as it does to this day. And below the surface of all the stories lies a deep wisdom about life, acquired through the ages, which has made these tales a work of art and part of the world's culture.

You will find in this collection a wide variety of tales — you will find romances, historic epics, adventure tales, travel stories, anecdotes and fables. They will give children of all ages many hours of enchantment.

Silent and still and full of fragrance were the starlit nights above the towns of the tall minarets, above the desert sands and sleeping caravans, above the caiques in the harbours.

This is how it has been since days of old. But in the days of the caliph Schahriar the night silence echoed with the voice of the beautiful Scheherazade, as she related her wondrous tales.

Who was Scheherazade?

It is written in the ancient book of fairy tales that she was the lovely and clever daughter of the grand vizier, who waited in dread for her to be chosen as their ruler's next bride. For the caliph, grieved at finding his first, his second and then his third wife deceitful and fickle, had had them all beheaded. And finally, to protect himself from such faithlessness, he wed each day a different maiden, and had each one executed the next morning.

Yet Scheherazade, heedless of the danger, wanted her turn to come, for she knew how to avoid the fearful fate of these maidens. She knew how to hold the caliph's attention. She told him tales, some merry, some sad, of good and evil, of wise and foolish men. All night she would speak, for not till the pale light of dawn did her master allow her to stop.

But never for long. Anxious to learn the end of the story, the caliph could hardly wait for the cool of the evening to return. Then he would sit and let the tales carry him to mysterious, unknown lands; he would laugh at the antics of the jesters, he would fear for the fate of the heroes and the heroines. And so it went on for a thousand and one nights...

Yet the words of the stories have remained for ever, just as the fragrance and the starlit nights have stayed above the towns of the tall minarets, above the desert sands and sleeping caravans, above the caiques in the harbours.

They are but a whisper, yet if we listen hard, we shall hear her voice just as the caliph heard it long ago.

Fate and Riches

Once a long time ago in Baghdad there lived two good friends, Sad and Sadi. Though Sadi was rich and Sad was as poor as a church mouse, they loved each other dearly. Neither would dream of doing a single thing without the other and they agreed on all questions except one. This one exception they argued about forever.

Sadi, the rich man believed that money could buy happiness.

"The more money a person has," he said, "the more independent of others he is, and the better and more comfortably he can live."

But Sad, the poor man thought differently. "Riches are useful and important enough," he would say, "but happiness is a matter of Fate. If Fate is against you, what good is money?"

"What nonsense!" Sadi objected. "Hard work and cleverness will bring riches, so anyone can guide his own fate."

Every time they met they argued about this matter. Then one day, as they were strolling together along a street in Baghdad, Sadi suddenly said:

"Let us find out which one of us is right. Hasan, the rope-maker lives nearby. He makes ropes from morning till night. But, as he has five children, he earns scarcely enough to keep them, his wife and himself alive. If I were to give him two hundred dinars, he could buy more flax and employ an assistant too. He would grow rich in no time at all. Surely you must see that he would then be happier!"

Sad was not convinced but agreed to test his friend's idea. And so the two went together into Hasan's shabby little shop.

"How long have you been a rope-maker, Hasan?" Sadi asked.

"All my life, sir," Hasan replied. "And this shop was my father's and my grandfather's before me."

"A very long time indeed," said Sadi. "But tell me, why is it that you can barely scrape a living?"

The rope-maker's face was full of sorrow.

"With the money I earn I can buy only very little flax for the next day. And what is left scarcely keeps hunger away from my door..."

"What if I were to give you, Hasan, two hundred dinars?" Sadi asked. "Would you spend them, or would you use them to make your business grow?"

"Oh, dear sir, if you truly mean what you say, then in no time at all I should become the richest rope-maker in Baghdad," Hasan answered.

Sadi smiled, and handing a purse to the rope-maker said, "Here are two hundred dinars exactly. In six months we shall return to see what changes for the better have occurred in your life."

Night had almost fallen, so Hasan closed the shop and hurried home. He wanted to hide the purse straight away in a safe place. But, alas, there was not a single cupboard or a single drawer in his poor little house. So he took out two dinars to buy a little food and wound the rest securely inside his turban.

He hurried off to the market to buy meat for supper. It had been so long since he, his wife or children had tasted good food. He chose a fine piece of

meat and feeling pleased and happy he started off for home. And as he walked he made all sorts of plans which would change his poor life.

But, alas! Just as he was nearing home and his head was full of wonderful ideas, a hungry vulture dived out of the darkening sky. It made straight for Hasan's supper. The rope-maker defended himself bravely against the claws of the thieving bird. But in the struggle his turban fell from his head to the ground. The vulture forgetting the meat, at once pounced on it. It screeched once and seizing the turban in its beak flew off. It was as if the evil bird knew that now it had caused far greater distress to Hasan.

The poor rope-maker almost burst into tears. All his wonderful dreams and plans had vanished in an instant. And what, he thought miserably, was

13

he going to say the kind rich man when he returned in six months?

Allah provided and Allah took away, Hasan said to himself at last with a deep sigh. And next morning he set to work again and toiled just as hard and for just as little as he had always done.

Sadi and Sad appeared in the rope-maker's shop exactly six months later. Hasan wasted no time in telling them of the misfortunes which had befallen him. As he listened Sadi kept shaking his head. He could not believe Hasan's story.

"But this man has a reputation for honesty," Sad defended him. "Surely you must see that I am right, that it is Fate that decides what is to be. Riches alone cannot bring happiness."

"I cannot agree with you," said Sadi, "but I shall give the rope-maker a second chance. Here are another 200 hundred dinars." And he tossed a second purse to Hasan. "Now," he said, "surely you can keep your promise. In three months' time I shall return to see for myself."

Sad and Sadi then went away, leaving Hasan on his knees, calling after them his words of thanks.

"This time I shall find a much safer hiding place for the money," Hasan promised himself. And he thought about it all the way home.

But the idea only came to him after he had shut the door behind him. In a corner stood an old jug filled with bran. This, he thought, was the ideal hiding place.

There was not a soul in the house, so quickly Hasan poured some of the bran out of the jug. Then putting the purse of dinars inside, he covered it over with bran.

Satisfied, Hasan hurried back to his shop. Little did he guess what was to happen that day.

In the middle of the afternoon a pedlar stopped at his door. He was selling clay powder which the wives of poor men used to wash their hair. Hasan's wife would like to have bought the powder,... but as she had not a single copper, she wondered what she could offer instead. Her glance fell upon the jug filled with bran. Such a thing was of no use to them at all. At last she persuaded the pedlar to take the jug in exchange for the powder. Who knows how far away the money was by the time the rope-maker returned home? Oh, how he groaned, how he mourned when he discovered what had happened. He blamed himself for keeping the whole affair secret from his wife. But more than anything he feared what Sadi and Sad would have to say when they returned.

The three months flew past like lightning and once again the two friends were standing before the miserable Hasan, waiting to hear his story.

"You're a good-for-nothing and a spendthrift," the rich Sadi shouted at the end. "I don't believe a single word of it."

But Sad only said, "Now you can see that riches will not win over Fate. I believe that it will take only a single copper to make this man happy. Rope-maker, please accept my gift this time, and do with it as you wish. We shall meet again in three months' time..."

The poor rope-maker was relieved that everything had gone so smoothly. He took the offered coin gratefully, and saw the two friends to the door with many bows and words of thanks.

He forgot all about the copper till late that evening, when a neighbour of his, who was a fisherman, called on him and asked, "Please, Hasan, lend

me just one copper. I need to have my nets mended before tomorrow morning..."

Why shouldn't one beggar help another? After all, whoever heard of anyone growing rich from one little coin?...

"Thank you for helping me, Hasan. Tomorrow my first catch shall be yours," said the fisherman, as he hurried out with his nets.

What a surprise was waiting for Hasan the next day: The fisherman came to him carrying in his arms a fish as long as a table.

"Never have I caught such a large fish," he laughed. "But it is yours, neighbour. It was the first one in my net."

Hasan did not want to accept such a fine gift, but the fisherman would not listen to his protests. So he thanked his neighbour and told his wife to cook the fish for supper.

Gladly his wife set to work. Suddenly she caught sight of something bright inside the fish. It shone like a fragment of coloured glass. The children saw it too and begged to be given the little glass to play with.

Their mother let them have it and off into the street they ran to show it to their friends. They played with their new toy until daylight had faded and the little glass gleamed and glittered in the darkness.

It so happened that a goldsmith was walking past and his eye was attracted by the glitter. He bent over the children to find out what they were playing with. He was amazed to see a magnificent diamond, more beautiful than any diamond he had ever seen. This time Fate was on Hasan's side. The goldsmith was an honest man, and he paid him one hundred thousand dinars for the precious stone.

The poor rope-maker was rich at last. Before the month was out, he had bought out every rope-making workshop in Baghdad. Outside the city he had a fine palace built in the centre of a beautiful park. Instead of a mean little shop, a large and grand building belonging to Hadji Hasan the Rope-Maker stood in the square.

When Sadi and Sad paid him a visit, they did not recognize the place. Only the familiar face of Hasan made them enter and listen to his tale.

Afterwards the grateful Hasan invited them both to visit his elegant palace outside the city. How they admired his splendid gardens full of flowers, trees, shrubs and birds from many lands.

But even now Sadi argued. "I really can't believe, my friend, that you have come to all these riches thanks to one single copper coin. To find a diamond inside a fish too is just as amazing as losing the four hundred

16

dinars before. Go on, own up that the money I gave you has helped you to this fortune!''

Hasan turned red at the injustice of this remark. The kindly Sad, seeing this, quickly began to praise Hasan's lovely garden, trying to cover up the awkward moment. Pointing to a nearby tree, he said, ''Look Hasan, not only have you the most unusual foreign plants, but also the most unusual nests.''

It was true — something white gleamed among the branches, something which no bird could have built. Hasan at once commanded his slaves to bring him the strange nest.

One glance was enough. He could scarcely believe his eyes. But it was indeed his old turban, the one the greedy vulture had carried off.

''At last here is proof that I have spoken the truth,'' he said, turning to

Sadi. "In this very turban your money is hidden." The rich man unwound the material. The dinars were still inside, just as Hasan knew they would be. Thereupon Hasan, Sad and Sadi too rejoiced at this happy find. And the good Sad hoped that surely now his friend would be convinced of Hasan's honesty.

But it was not so. As all three were returning to Baghdad on horseback, Sadi turned to Hasan once more.

"By bread and salt, which are the mark of our brotherhood, tell me the truth. Did you not find the second purse of two hundred dinars helpful in making your fortune?"

What could Hasan reply? He was filled with bitterness at Sadi's lack of faith in his word. But little did he dream that his truthfulness would soon be proved a second time.

It was dead of night when at last they reached Baghdad. The horses were worn out and hungry. Fodder must be found at once for the poor beasts.

The whole town was asleep and for a time they searched in vain. At last a slave returned to Hasan, his master. In his hands he carried an old jug.

"This is the only thing I could find, my master. And I fear the bran it holds is old but the whole town has closed down till morning."

But Hasan stopped him. He recognized that old jug.

"Put your hand into this jug, Sadi," he commanded. "Surely you will recognize your own purse."

And so for a second time the rich man was convinced. At last he had to agree with his friend Sad. "Riches do not lead to riches. Only the will of Allah, written in the Book of Destinies, decides what is to be will be."

Aladdin and his Magic Lamp

Somewhere in the depths of Africa there once lived a powerful magician, who possessed much worldly treasure. In the main, he came by this through practising wicked sorcery. One day he was sitting as usual in front of his strange instruments and magic books with which he could look into the future. Suddenly he saw amidst a whirl of mist something that made him gasp for breath.

In a far away town it seems there lived a young lad called Aladdin who without knowing it himself, possessed great magic power. What was more,

20

buried deep in a cave below a little hill outside the town was the most wonderful treasure in all the world. That was not all. In the very same cave there was an old lamp which could fulfill every wish. Aladdin and Aladdin only could reach the treasure and the lamp.

The magician, at first quite dazed by what he saw, suddenly came back to earth. Was he not a great magician? he asked himself. Most certainly he would not allow some young unknown rascal to possess such treasure.

Hastily he disguised himself as a holy man. Then twisting the ring he wore on his finger, he spoke:

"Take me to the town where the boy Aladdin lives!"

In a trice he found himself far, far away, in the very street where Aladdin was playing with his companions. As soon as the magician had singled out the boy, he called to him:

"Aladdin, my dear nephew! Come here, so that I may embrace you! I have been searching so long for you."

The lad gazed at the strange man in astonishment, and then answered:

"I do not know you, sir, and my mother has never told me about an uncle. My father when he was alive did not mention you either."

"Alas, my poor brother!" the artful magician cried, covering his face with his hands as if he were deeply grieved. "We had not seen each other for so long, and now you tell me that he lives no longer. Dear Aladdin," he continued turning to the boy, "because of the love I had for your dear father, I want to take care of your education and make you into a fine gentleman. Judging by the clothes you are wearing, your mother has little money to spare."

"You are right, Uncle. My mother is only a poor spinner," Aladdin admitted sadly. "Let us go and find her and tell her the happy news."

At first the widow did not like or trust the mysterious stranger, but after a time she began to believe what he said, particularly when he handed her ten gold dinars to buy clothes for her son.

"Buy only the best, dear sister-in-law," the magician instructed her as he departed. "If Aladdin's destiny lies among the rich and the powerful, he must dress accordingly. I shall judge for myself tomorrow, for I will begin his education first thing in the morning."

The widow did not grudge her son the money, and spent every dinar to the last copper on fine new clothes.

The following morning, when the stranger returned, Aladdin was waiting for him dressed as grandly as any rich man's son.

"Your mother has done well," the magician approved. "Now let us not waste any time. The sooner we leave, the more you will learn."

He then took the boy to the most enchanting gardens. They were full of strange and beautiful flowers in full bloom and their scent perfumed the air. These blooms of many colours were mirrored in ponds and little lakes whose bottoms were inlaid with gay mosaic patterns and whose surfaces were adorned with countless sparkling fountains. They strolled upon lawns as smooth and soft as velvet and the air above trembled with the song of birds. Such sights and sounds Aladdin had never seen even in his dreams. As he looked at Aladdin who was lost in wonder the magician rubbed his hands together with satisfaction. His wicked plans would go well, he thought.

"Now I want to show you a place which will truly amaze you," he told Aladdin. "No man alive has ever before seen such magnificence and riches," he promised the boy as they neared the hill under which the treasure lay hidden. "But first wait."

The magician then began to measure the ground by pacing a few steps in one direction, and a few paces in another. At last he stopped. Lighting a few dry twigs which he had gathered he threw a handful of incense upon them. Soon a cloud of smoke hid Aladdin and the magician from sight.

"Look down through the smoke," said the magician, pointing to the ground. Aladdin was amazed to see a boulder with an iron ring fixed to it.

"Only you can lift this stone and descend into the depths of the earth," his false uncle whispered. "You will walk through passages and halls, and along garden paths. Whatever you see on the way, whatever you find will be yours. The one thing which I desire is a lighted lamp that hangs there."

"I will go with pleasure, Uncle," Aladdin agreed. "But why will you not come too?"

"I shall wait here, to make sure of your safe return," lied the magician, feigning concern. "Now go at once."

So Aladdin grasped the iron ring and pulled it up so easily, that the magician gasped in surprise.

The boy went along a dark passage which led into a series of vast halls filled with gold, silver, diamonds, pearls and other precious stones. Without knowing it, Aladdin had discovered the greatest treasure in the world.

He hastened on, however, till the passage widened and he entered a garden which was more like a dream. The branches of the trees were so heavily laden that they bent over with fruit. But these were no ordinary

22

fruits. They dazzled the eye with a blaze of colour. Glittering diamonds, lily-white pearls, deep red rubies, violet amethysts, green emeralds and blue sapphires hung from every branch. Even the petals of the flowers were of the finest gold, fine enough to adorn the head of any princess. And there too in a niche in the garden hung the lamp which Aladdin sought. It was old, it was dirty and it shone dully.

The boy took it down very carefully. He put out the flame, poured away the oil and set out on his return journey. Only then did he allow himself to look round and admire what he saw. He also filled his pockets with a few of the wondrous riches which were everywhere.

The magician was waiting for him with the utmost impatience. The moment he saw Aladdin, he cried, "What a long time you have taken. Come now, pass up the lamp to me, then I will help you up."

"Oh, Uncle, I can't, the lamp is heavy. Give me your hand and help me up first," Aladdin begged.

The magician, however, had no intention of helping Aladdin. He only wanted the lamp, and meant to be rid of the boy. So he repeated his demand. He pleaded, he cajoled, he threatened — but all in vain. Aladdin tried again and again but he could not push the lamp through the narrow opening. At last, the magician flew into the most terrible rage.

"You ungrateful boy," he roared. "I'll teach you a lesson." And with these words he tossed another handful of incense onto the fire, muttering at the same time some magic words in a strange tongue. The stone with the iron ring began to move. Slowly, slowly it came to rest in its original place over the opening.

"You fool! If I cannot have the lamp, I shall leave you to die. No one will ever find you," the magician cried, with a wicked laugh. And with a twist of the magic ring on his finger he was gone.

Aladdin was all alone in the darkness. How could he have guessed that his newly found uncle would treat him so cruelly? He called and he cried out, but no one could hear him, and he soon realized that escape was impossible without help. He ran back along the passage, through the halls and into the garden, in search of another way out. But there was none. Hopelessly he came back to the top of the passage.

Miserably, he sank down in a dark corner and shed silent tears. Clasping his hands together, he whispered the words of a prayer. As he prayed he unwittingly rubbed his hand across the surface of the old lamp. Suddenly, an enormous genie stood before him.

"You called me, master. What is your wish?" he asked, bowing low before Aladdin.

"Take me to my mother!" the boy commanded, dazed with surprise. Before he could recover from his astonishment, Aladdin was standing in front of his own house.

After he had told his mother the full story of his adventures, they both realized that great magic was hidden in the old lamp. So this was why the magician had wanted the lamp for himself! they said to each other.

"Now we no longer need fear poverty!" Aladdin rejoiced, and to prove it, he rubbed the lamp. The genie appeared at once and Aladdin ordered him to serve supper. The genie disappeared, returning in an instant carrying a large silver tray laden with twelve silver dishes, each one filled to the brim with the choicest foods. There were goblets with fine wines, exotic fruit and white bread. This feast was placed before Aladdin and his astonished mother. She could hardly believe her eyes. Then she began to tremble with fear.

"Throw away that lamp, my son. It has evil powers and will bring you no good."

"Why, mother, it is this very power which has set me free from the trap my wicked uncle had set for me," Aladdin protested, and began to eat hungrily. But the widow remained worried, unable to chase away her fears.

To please his mother, Aladdin promised that for the time being he would hide the lamp away in a safe place and look for some honest work. But for quite some time they lived comfortably from the sale of the silver dishes and the silver tray.

By day, Aladdin would stroll through the markets, watching the goldsmiths, merchants and traders at work. He talked to them too and tried to learn something of their skills.

Finally one day he decided to go into business on his own. Taking the precious jewels he had brought from the underground cave, he left the house. He had not gone far when the blare of trumpets stopped him. Aladdin heard the voice of the sultan's herald.

"Make way, make way! It is the command of the sultan, who honours us by being our ruler, that you all return instantly to your homes, and close your doors and windows firmly. Our princess will shortly pass this way and must not be seen. If anyone dares to disobey this command, he will lose his head instantly."

Aladdin had heard many times about the beauty of the Princess Badralbudur, and now he was filled with the strongest desire to see her face. So heedless of the danger, he hid in the shadows of a doorway and waited for her to pass by.

Even from a distance Princess Badralbudur outshone all the maidens round her. She stood in beauty like a flower surrounded by blades of grass. As she passed Aladdin's doorway, she slightly raised the veil from her face. Her radiant loveliness struck Aladdin's heart with such force that he collapsed to the ground in a swoon.

Not till the evening did he come to his senses, then still in a trance he picked up his jewels and turned towards home. The vision of the princess stayed before his eyes, and though his common sense told him it was madness, his heart yearned for her.

He could not eat or sleep and soon his mother realized something was amiss. She persuaded Aladdin to confide in her.

"Alas, my son, whatever shall we do?" she cried, when he had told her of his love. "The sultan's daughter was never meant for someone like you. Whatever can you be thinking of! Put such nonsense out of your head at once."

"My fortune can equal the sultan's fortune," Aladdin replied in his own defence. "I may be the son of a poor tailor, but I am sure our ruler does not have in his coffers jewels such as these..."

Aladdin uncovered the basin which held his jewels, and continued, "You yourself, dear mother, must go to the sultan and ask him on my behalf for the princess Badralbudur's hand in marriage. Take these jewels with you as a present from me. Please don't refuse me, for otherwise I shall die with longing."

There is nothing a mother would not do for her son. So the widow summoned her courage, picked up the dish with the jewels and went to the palace. She passed through the gates and into the divan — a large spacious hall, which was crowded with noble lords, viziers and judges of the sultan's court. In the centre upon his throne, sat the sultan himself. He was hearing and judging pleas from his subjects and issuing his decisions and commands to which the plaintiffs listened humbly.

As she watched the widow almost lost heart. She was about to steal away when the sultan noticed her.

"Bring that woman to me, I wish to know what she is doing here," he cried.

The widow fell to her knees, kissing the floor at the sultan's feet, and spoke. "Your Majesty, I beg your forgiveness! I beg you to pardon the impudent request with which I come to you."

"Rise, woman," the sultan replied quite kindly. "You have my promise that not a single hair of your head shall be harmed. Do not be shy. Tell me why you are here."

"I have a son, Aladdin," the widow began, and in a tremulous voice went on to tell him how her son, though forbidden to do so, had seen the beauty of the princess and had fallen madly in love with her. "This is why I am here, Your Majesty, to ask for the princess's hand in marriage for my son."

"And what makes this impudent fellow think himself worthy of my daughter?" asked the sultan laughing.

"He sends you this gift," the widow replied bravely, and uncovered the dish which held the jewels. The whole divan hummed with admiration. Everyone gasped with amazement and the sultan leant over to his grand vizier and said:

"Every one of these jewels is more valuable than anything I have in my treasury. What do you say to such a gift? What answer should I give?"

"I must admit that such jewels are worthy of the princess," the grand vizier agreed reluctantly. "But," he added, "I think it would be wise if you made him wait three months for the wedding. I feel a little suspicious as to the means by which such a fellow comes to possess such riches. I should like to look into this matter most carefully."

"Go home, good woman," the sultan said to the widow, "and tell your Aladdin that I shall be happy to grant him his request. But he must be patient and agree to wait for three months, for it will take that time to make all the preparations for the wedding festivities." So saying, the sultan dismissed the widow.

The mother, overjoyed at such tidings, hurried home to tell her son the good news. That night Aladdin fell asleep with his heart brimming with happiness and full of thanks to Allah.

He did not dream that the grand vizier would do his utmost to prevent him from marrying Princess Badralbudur. For he too had a son, and it was his intention that he and not Aladdin, would marry the princess and sit one day on the sultan's throne. Had not the sultan almost promised his daughter to the boy long before Aladdin had been heard of? Was he going to allow the son of a poor tailor to spoil all his plans?

The vizier knew exactly what to do. The sultan was getting old and forgetful and as there was no mention of Aladdin's name for some time, the sultan forgot the promise he had made. Eventually the artful vizier managed to convince his master that his own son was most worthy to marry Princess Badralbudur.

The vizier then wasted no time in making preparations for the wedding celebrations. The most important of these was to be a grand procession through the city to the sultan's palace.

The great day dawned. Mounted soldiers and guards in ceremonial uniform rode through the streets, while the people lit bright lamps in their windows and tossed a thousand flowers at the procession.

Aladdin knew nothing of this, for he had scarcely left his little room. He had spent the time impatiently counting the days which remained to the end of the three months.

But that particular evening he ventured into the streets and was amazed at what he saw.

"You cannot be a local man," someone remarked. "Today we are celebrating the wedding of the grand vizier's son and our Princess Badralbudur. As soon as the bridegroom comes out of the bath house we will all accompany him to the palace..."

Aladdin did not listen further. He turned on his heel and hurried home as fast as he could. He burst into his room, took out the lamp which he had hidden away in a safe place and rubbed its surface with the palm of his hand.

"What is your command, master?" asked the genie, bowing low before him.

"At this very moment the wedding procession is on its way to Princess Badralbudur at her father's palace. It is my wish to take the place of the bridegroom. Carry the vizier's son to his father's house and lock him up there. I must also be dressed in identical clothes!"

"Your wish will be carried out," replied the slave of the lamp. In the twinkling of an eye Aladdin was rubbed with perfumed oils, clad in magnificent royal robes and transported to the palace.

The procession had already reached the gates and nobody noticed the exchange take place, so cleverly did the genie carry out Aladdin's commands.

Only the sultan and the grand vizier gazed in astonishment at the face of the mysterious stranger. Aladdin threw himself at the sultan's feet.

"Most honoured Monarch, I come according to the promise you gave my mother," Aladdin spoke.

The sultan turned angrily to the grand vizier.

"Now I remember... this must be Aladdin. But you, grand vizier, you wanted to put your son in his place. You have deceived me."

"I was only thinking of your good, Master," the sly vizier said in his own defence, furious at this unexpected turn of events. "And if you take my advice, you will demand from the bridegroom a dowry worthy of the princess. Why, you do not even know how this young man earns a living."

The sultan thought for a moment, then said aloud,

"It has always been our custom, Aladdin, to expect a rich dowry for a princess. For Badralbudur I demand forty dishes made of pure gold, filled to the brim with jewels. Otherwise you will not wed my only daughter".

"Have patience for just one moment, Your Majesty," the youth replied boldly, and added to the astonishment of all present, "I will return presently with the dowry you demand."

Quickly he returned to his house. Moments later he appeared in the street leading a procession of forty lovely maidens, each one carrying on her head a gold dish filled to the brim with the most priceless jewels. All this Aladdin had obtained with the aid of the magic lamp.

What a magnificent procession made its way to the palace! Aladdin rode in front, astride a magnificent Arabian stallion, followed by his mother, dressed like a true queen and accompanied by a dozen female slaves. Other attendants followed on horseback, tossing handfuls of gold coins to the crowds who lined the streets.

At first the sultan could hardly believe his eyes. Then stepping forward to meet Aladdin, he embraced him warmly and greeted him as his own son. He no longer needed the warnings of the jealous grand vizier.

This was the signal for the festivities to begin.

In an instant the air was alive with the sound of music and the ground trembled with a thousand dancing feet. The whole palace was ablaze with light and everyone rejoiced, feasted and sang. The sultan liked Aladdin at once. He called forth his judges and ordered them to draw up the wedding contract. When this was done, Aladdin rose and begged permission to leave. "Where do you want to go, my son? This is the day of your wedding. Your bride awaits you," the puzzled sultan asked.

"Her beauty is such that she deserves more than I have given her so far," Aladdin answered. "I have decided that before daybreak I shall build a palace fit to receive a princess. I should be grateful if you yourself would select the spot where you wish us to live."

"Choose any of my land you desire, if you think it necessary," the sultan replied. "But," he added, "you do not have to build your own palace. From this day my palace is yours."

An invisible army of genies toiled all through that night building a palace not far distant from the sultan's own. They gathered together vast quantities of the finest marble, jasper, agate; the rooms were fitted with silver and gold, magnificent materials draped the walls, the floors were inlaid with mosaic and before the break of day the passages buzzed with the voices of servants, the clatter of dishes floated from the kitchens and the stamping of horses' hooves from the stables. And as the sun came up a brocade carpet was being laid all the way from the steps to the sultan's palace. This was the very last task Aladdin had given the slave of the magic lamp.

It is almost impossible to describe the magnificence and the joy that attended the wedding of Aladdin and the princess. Most important of all, Badralbudur fell in love with her husband as deeply as he was in love with her. The sly grand vizier, seeing that his cause was lost for ever, did not try again to mar their happiness.

From that day they would have lived happily to the end of the story, if the wicked magician had not thought of Aladdin again. He was living in the heart of darkest Africa when one day it suddenly occurred to him that perhaps he could try once again to get the magic lamp. At the same time

31

he would try to find out whether the youth, whom he had imprisoned in the cavern, had indeed perished.

So he shut himself in his chamber with his books and instruments. Upon chanting certain secret formulae, the magician was astounded to discover that Aladdin was now living like a king and that the beautiful Badralbudur, the daughter of the sultan himself, was his wife.

The magician flew into a terrible fury. He spat and fumed as if possessed by a thousand devils. But while he cursed and raged, he was thinking hard how he could get his hands on that precious lamp — for he was quite sure that the son of the poor tailor could not have become the son-in-law of the sultan without the help of the lamp's magic powers.

Once he had decided to act, he did not waste another minute. Twisting the ring on his finger, he had himself transported to the capital of China.

Before long he was strolling through the streets and as he strolled he asked questions. He soon learned the whereabouts of Aladdin's palace. Before going there, however, he did a surprising thing. He bought several beautiful new lamps, and as he walked he called "a new lamp for your old, a new lamp for your old..."

No one could understand such foolishness and many people hastened to take advantage of this strange bargain. The magician exchanged the lamps with a smile, and all the time he was getting nearer and nearer to Aladdin's palace. By the time he came to the gates he had only one new lamp left.

"New lamps for old, new lamps for old!" he cried, looking up at the windows. "I will exchange my last new lamp for your old one!" He had found out that Aladdin and the princess were not in the palace, so he did not fear discovery. He could hardly breathe for excitement when one of the palace slaves leaned out of a window and called,

"Wait a moment, trader! Our master has a very old and ugly lamp in his bedroom; I am sure he will be glad to exchange it for a new one."

The magician could hardly believe his luck. It was the very lamp he had longed to have in his possession. Giving the slave a new lamp in exchange, he hastily crept out of town. Then he hid and waited for night to fall when everyone would be asleep.

Darkness came. The magician grasped the lamp in one hand and rubbed it hard with the other. At once the genie appeared before him.

"What is your command, master?" he asked with a bow.

"You are to take up Aladdin's palace and transport it with the princess in it to my home in the depths of Africa. But you are to leave Aladdin here.

32

The sultan himself will deal with him." And the magician laughed evilly...

The night was without stars, without a moon; only the gale howled and moaned above the town. All of a sudden, unseen by anyone in the city, Aladdin's palace with all its turrets and domes rose into the sky just as the magician had commanded, leaving nothing but barren ground in its place.

The next day, as soon as the old sultan awoke and rubbed his eyes, he looked across, as was his custom, at Aladdin's palace. But today! He could not believe his eyes. Was he still dreaming? Alas, no! It was as if a mighty wind had blown, removing all in its path. Where the palace had stood there was an empty space. Horrified, the old sultan summoned his grand vizier.

"Tell me what you see," he commanded, pushing him to the window. "Tell me it is only a dream."

"Oh Your Majesty, the palace has gone!" cried the vizier, stuttering with amazement. Then drawing himself up, he turned to the sultan. "Sire," he said. "if only my words of warning had not fallen on deaf cars. I have always feared that impudent youth, Aladdin, had succeeded in wedding your lovely daughter by foul means and dishonest magic! We must catch him, punish him severely, and force him to explain his awful purpose. Only the night before the sultan had sung Aladdin's praises. Now he could find nothing but harsh words to say about him.

"He will suffer the worst tortures," he cried in a voice full of rage and misery. "Let the guards search every corner of the town and gardens..."

They did not have to search for long. Aladdin was sound asleep under the nearest bush, and when he found himself dragged before the angry sultan, he did not understand what had happened. Not until he was thrown into the deepest dungeon did he find out why he was a prisoner. By then

34

he could no longer help himself, or defend himself. From far above he could just hear the voice of the sultan.

"I shall let you stay alive for just forty days and forty nights, but if Badralbudur does not return by then I shall give you to the executioner..."

His heart heavy with grief Aladdin heard those words. Who was sorrier than he at the loss of his dearest princess? He thought long and hard about her mysterious disappearance and about the disappearance of their palace. He finally realized that only the wicked magician could be responsible for bringing them to this plight. But how could he get the better of the magician, who now must have the magic lamp in his possession?

While Aladdin was suffering in prison the wicked magician was strutting before the weeping princess Badralbudur.

"You weep in vain, most beautiful princess, for you will never see Aladdin again!" he gloated. "I have had you carried in your palace all the way here to Africa. There is not a man alive who would dare to try and steal you from me now. You are my chosen bride and this evening I shall come to ask you for your hand. If you refuse me, may heaven help you, for no man will," he added threateningly, as he withdrew.

The princess hid her face in her hands. But unlike Aladdin, who was now powerless against the powers of the magic lamp, she at last thought of a plan. It was a very clever plan indeed.

That evening she dressed herself in her most beautiful robes, rubbed the most expensive scented ointments into her skin, and ordered the table to be laden with heady wines, succulent food and fruits. Then she sat down and waited for the magician. She greeted him with a smile.

"At last you have come, my master," she whispered, kneeling before him.
The magician could not take his eyes off her.

"I can see you have thought over my proposal..." he began, but Badralbudur did not let him finish. She invited him to join her at the table and filled his glass with wine. She laughed and joked, talked a lot of sweet nonsense, and as the evening turned to night, the magician emptied one glass after another. The princess hardly moistened her lips.

"I am well aware, my master, that your power is greater than the combined power of all the kings. Tell me where does it come from?" she asked, at last.

"From this lamp," stuttered the magician, taking the lamp from his robe with an unsteady hand. "I need only rub the palm of my hand over it and..." He was never to finish his sentence. Suddenly he slid gently to the floor and started to snore loudly. This was what the princess had been waiting for. She grasped the lamp and began to rub her hand over it.

"What is your command, my mistress?" asked the genie, who was so huge, so frightening, that at first Badralbudur was terrified.

"Take this black-hearted magician to hell, where he belongs, and return immediately!" she said, gaining courage.

The giant genie immediately lifted up the magician as if he were a wisp of straw, and disappeared. A moment later he was back.

"The magician will never be seen on this earth again," he said. "What is your next command, Princess?"

"Let this palace stand where it stood before!"

The lamp had always made every wish come true, and its magic did not fail the princess. Long before cock crow, Aladdin was released from prison, reunited with his princess and they and the sultan rejoiced together. The evil they had suffered was soon forgotten.

But on that day the magic lamp disappeared and was never seen again. The clever princess had broken it into little pieces. Some she burned, some she buried and the rest she cast into the sea.

She did this because she feared human envy, wickedness and the desire for power, for they can often be stronger than goodness.

The Stolen Purse

Four merchants once happened to meet on a caravan trail in the desert. As they were all going in the same direction, they decided to travel on together. But as none had met before, they did not trust one another. Nevertheless, for the time they were to be together, they agreed to put their money in a common purse, which they all then guarded carefully, for it contained one thousand dinars!

When they came to the nearest town, they found on the outskirts a most beautiful garden in which to rest.

Dismounting, they handed their beasts to the old woman who sat at the gate. They also gave her the purse with the words,

"You are to return this purse to us only when all four of us come back together."

Then, thankfully they sank into the shade of the almond bushes. Once rested, they were so tempted by the cool clear waters of a small pool in the garden that all four of them jumped in and splashed and played about in it like little children. Soon their beards and hair were wet and tangled.

"I will go to the old woman and borrow a comb," offered the youngest merchant who was only just out of his teens. He dressed speedily, so that no one would try to stop him and spoil his plan.

"Give me the purse. The others have sent me for it," he said to the old woman at the gate, pretending to look important and older than he was.

"Not so fast, my lad! First I must consult your companions!" the old woman replied, and as the pond was in sight and within earshot, she placed her hand to her mouth and shouted, "Shall I give it to him?"

The merchants in the water thought she meant the comb, so they replied, "Why ever not? We sent him to fetch it!"

And as they continued to splash in the water, the thief was galloping off in a cloud of dust with the money.

It was much later when the others noticed his absence. Full of suspicion, they ran to the old woman.

Much too late they realized their mistake. By then the young scoundrel was far away. But they were not going to give up so easily. Gripping the old woman by the elbows, they led her to a local judge.

"This old hag is in our debt, sir," spoke the eldest merchant and

continued in his accusation. "We placed a purse with a thousand gold dinars in her safe keeping, on condition that she would return it only if all four of us came back for it. But she gave it to the youngest one of us and he ran away with the money. We were unable to catch him!"

"Is that how it was?" the judge asked the old woman.

"Yes, Your Worship," she replied, her head bowed.

"In that case you must return the purse, or you will be punished!" the judge pronounced.

"I shall return it gladly," said the old woman, looking straight at the merchants. "But only on condition that all four of them come for it — as was agreed!"

"That too is my final decision," said the protector of law. "Find your fellow-traveller, and you shall get the purse. But until you do, this woman in front of you shall remain blameless."

So the merchants discovered that though it appears easy to put the blame on an innocent person, it is without doubt much better to catch the real culprit.

The Beautiful Maryam

Masrur was not a wealthy merchant, but a handsome man into the bargain. And as he knew how to benefit most from both these gifts fate had given him, he was very successful in buying and selling, enjoyed life to the full and was very popular with all the beautiful maidens of the town. There was only one matter which caused argument between him and those around him, and that was his faith, for unlike them he had become a Christian.

One day when he had gone out for a walk, he found himself strolling through gardens scented with blossom. There he saw a maiden who was a vision of loveliness. He did not know, he had not dreamed that such beauty existed. The graceful charm of this enchanting stranger caught and held his glance, and at that moment his heart was fired with the flame of love.

Masrur greeted this exquisite being and remained talking to her in the gardens. He found it impossible to tear himself away, although the maiden remained aloof.

They ate and drank together, then Maryam — for that was her name — invited him to play a game of chess. Masrur played carelessly and badly, for his brain, which normally was so clear, was dazed by the love he felt for Maryam. The girl then suggested that they play for money. Did she perhaps wish to force him to concentrate on the game?

Masrur accepted the suggestion gladly, and they continued to play. But that day he lost all the money he had with him.

"Permit me to have another game tomorrow," he said to the girl, as she was putting the chessboard away. She agreed, but as she bade him good night, she advised him:

"Do not let all you have been endowed with slip through your fingers, for whatever happens, I shall never be yours."

Masrur did not heed her words of warning, but soon they were to come true. On the second day he lost all his money, on the third day his shop and his goods, and on the fourth his house and fields were gone too. But even the loss of all his property did not bring him to his senses.

Instead he said to the girl, "For the fourth day now you have allowed me to feast my eyes upon your beauty, and you have enraptured my heart more and more. During these four days I have become penniless through my bad play; but how unimportant that is compared with the knowledge that tomorrow I shall not see you again! Please tell me what I can bring with me tomorrow so that I may spend a fifth day with you?"

"Bring me amber, musk and four gowns made of the finest brocade," replied Maryam, knowing well that Masrur did not have a single dinar left with which to buy such expensive gifts.

But the merchant went straight into the streets. He knew many people, he had many friends. Each time he met a friend, he was glad to help Masrur and lent him whatever he asked.

So Masrur was able to visit his chosen one even on the fifth day. But this time they did not continue their game of chess. Instead Maryam listened to the voice of Masrur reciting verses which praised her loveliness and gloried in his love which flowed right from his heart.

Now Maryam could see that his love was true and eternal and because everything she had done before was only done to prove his sincerity she now admitted her own love for him which she had hidden so well and for so many days.

Maryam returned to Masrur all that she had won, and now for them both began the most enchanting time in their lives. They passed it in the scented gardens from morn till night. Their love was so strong they found it almost unbearable to be parted for a moment.

Alas, unhappy days were in store for them. One day Maryam's slave Hububa rushed to Masrur with bad tidings.

"Oh master, I dread to tell you that the old Jew, who is Maryam's husband, is returning home!"

The blood drained from Masrur's face. He hastened to his beloved. To his joy she related to him a plan which would allow them to continue seeing each other.

"When my husband starts working at the market, you must steal into his

favour," she told to him. "Then all will be as it was before, for he will be sure to invite you into his house…"

And so it came about. The Jew arrived home, and on the very first day as he displayed his wares in the market, he and Masrur met. It was not long before Masrur had persuaded him to take him as a business partner. Soon afterwards the Jew brought him into his house, though Maryam pretended not to care to have a guest.

It seemed that everything would continue as before, and that the old Jew would not discover about their great love. This would probably have been so, but not for the thousand-voiced lark, which the Jew had kept in his home for many years.

For the bird had become accustomed not to have its old master about when he had gone on his travels and it had made friends with Masrur. And now the lark would perch on his head, or shoulder and would allow Masrur to catch and hold it, whereas it would not go near the Jew. And as he was a suspicious old man who knew his beautiful young wife had been unwilling to marry him, it did not take him long to realize the truth.

But he soon discovered that their love was strong and it would not be easy to part them. And so he decided to take Maryam to a far away land where Masrur could not reach them.

Secretly he sold all his wares, secretly he prepared the caravan, and one day as dawn was breaking, he set Maryam and her slave Hububa on camels and started with them on the long journey.

They travelled for days, they travelled for weeks, for months, till a whole year went by, and the Jew continued to lead them from place to place, for it soon became apparent that even the greatest distance is not an obstacle to true love. Whenever it was possible, Maryam wrote, sending her letters by the few caravans they happened to meet along the route, and she received news from Masrur in the same way.

Eventually the Jew decided that he would handcuff his wife and her slave. He made them take off their costly garments and dressed them instead in dirty old rags, smearing their skins with sulphur smoke to make them look like the meanest of slaves.

Next he led them to a blacksmith and ordered him to make strong handcuffs, threatening at the same time that if he dared to refuse, he would see to it that he lost all his money.

But the blacksmith was much more impressed by Maryam's beautiful face than by the Jew's threats. When he found himself alone with the girl,

he asked, "Tell me, how did this come about? Why do you have to endure being humiliated by such an ugly old man?"

"You are the very first person to show interest in the fate of a humble creature like myself," Maryam replied, "but even your strength is not enough to alter what is to be..."

"Confess, dear young lady, tell me all," the blacksmith insisted, for he was spellbound by her delicate beauty. "Even a simple blacksmith may have a few influential friends who would gladly help you."

"Listen then: My father once placed a small fortune in the Jew's hands. He promised to enlarge it through his business. But soon afterwards my father died, and I was left to try and get our fortune back. I took my slave Hububa to help me, but for a long time we searched for the swindler in vain. At last we caught up with him just outside this town. There he tried to force me into marrying him and convert me to his faith. When I refused to agree to his suggestions, he flew into a terrible rage, destroyed the written agreement he once made with my father, and pronounced that from then on we were his slaves. This is why you have been asked to make the handcuffs."

The astonished blacksmith believed every word Maryam spoke. He handcuffed the two maidens in front of the Jew so that he would not be suspicious, than he ran to the chief judge in the town and told him everything he had heard.

In the name of justice, and also because he was curious to see for himself the young woman whose beauty, according to the blacksmith, no other could match, compelled the judge to summon the jury for the very next day to hear this case.

The Jew was visiting friends in the town, so Maryam was able to dress in proper clothes which enhanced her beauty all the more. Scenting herself with musk, she left for the court with the blacksmith, who had meantime unlocked her bonds.

Once there, to make sure she would please the chief judge and his three assistant judges, Maryam promised each one of them that she would marry him if only she was set free.

How could her case fail?

The bailiffs caught up with the unsuspecting Jew, thrashed him, and took him to the court by force, so that he would hear the verdict with his own ears. His hands and feet would be chopped off, the judge pronounced, if he did not allow Maryam to be free in faith and in rights and if he did not return to her all the property which since her father's death was rightly hers. In the end the Jew agreed with everything and was glad to escape with a whole skin.

His wife in the meantime gathered all her most valuable possessions and swiftly left the town with Hububa. It was high time too — for it did not take long for the four lovesick judges to meet. And it is said, that when everything became clear to them, their hearts suffered such a blow that shortly afterwards they all passed away.

By then Maryam and Hububa were on their way home.

After many weeks of wandering Maryam and Hububa at last reached their home town. Masrur could hardly believe his eyes when he saw his beloved alive and well and even lovelier than before. He had been almost ready to bid life goodbye, so long had it been since he had heard news of her.

But Maryam's arrival poured fresh strength into his weakened body. And because Masrur realized that only the true God was responsible for this renewed, unexpected happiness, he changed to the Moslem faith. With Maryam he had a wedding agreement prepared, and very soon they would become husband and wife.

But once again danger crossed their path. One day Hububa met the old Jew in the street. He was going home as fast as he could, he said, and was looking forward to paying Maryam back in full for what she had done. But the quick-thinking Hububa's face saddened with grief, and she sobbed, "My dear master, you would be seeking my mistress in vain. When you took so long to return, her heart burst with anguish — she passed away but

a few days ago. I am just on my way to the cemetery. If you like, come with me and I will show you her grave."

The Jew did not believe Hububa to begin with, but he followed her all the same. Once in the cemetery, the slave led him to a new grave where she started to cry so pitifully that the old man's doubts vanished and he too wept bitterly — for he also loved Maryam sincerely. And because he was old and full of grief and shame, he collapsed and died there at the graveside.

So Maryam and Masrur were safe at last and from that day no one tried to rob them of their happiness.

Maruf and the Ugly Fatima

There lived, in the old city of Cairo, two boys whose fathers' houses shared the same wall in Red Street by Zuvail Gate. Maruf and Ali were their names and they were close friends and constant companions.

Together they got up to many of the usual childish pranks, but one day they went too far; they took it into their heads to dress up like the sons of the Christians, and then to enter a Christian church, and steal several prayer books, sell them later to purchase sweets and trinkets with the money.

50

The young scoundrels robbed the church several times, but one day they were caught in the act by the Christians, who complained bitterly to the boys' families. Ali's father Ahman, who was a simple man, wasted no words, but gave his son such a beating that Ali, after such shame and dishonour, fled from the town, and no one knew where to find him.

Maruf had to go on living and growing up in the pleasant city without his dear friend. It was written in the book of life that when he grew up, his destiny would be to become a cobbler and to marry Fatima.

And so it happened. No one could possibly say that his wife was renowned for her beauty, or for her goodness of heart, or for her gentleness. On the contrary, she was famed for ugliness, bad temper and a wicked tongue, so it was no wonder she bore the nickname of Ugly Fatima. Poor Maruf! His days and nights were filled with harassment, worry and fear, particularly whenever he happened to leave his cobbler's shop with next to no money.

One day Fatima fancied kunaf noodles with bees' honey poured over them. But as luck would have it, that very day Maruf did not have a single customer. So that night he closed his shop with a heavy heart and fearful misgivings, dreading the reception which would surely be waiting for him at home.

He slouched along as slowly as he dared. His steps led him past the kunaf stall, and when he saw the pile of noodles, which for him were an unobtainable luxury, his eyes brimmed with tears. When the kunaf seller asked the reason for the tears, Maruf poured out all his fears and worries.

The kind kunaf seller then proceeded to weigh five whole pounds of kunaf, to fry it in clarified butter and saturate it with drip honey. It looked and smelled good enough to be served to a king.

Then he said to Maruf, "As you can see, I have no bees' honey, but I have used drip honey from the sugar cane, which is tastier anyway. Go home now, take the sweet to your wife and make her happy. I will gladly wait for your money till God helps you to better earnings."

Maruf took the kunaf most gratefully, and hastened home, murmuring his thanks. Anyone would think that Fatima would have been pleased...

Not in the least. Maruf was in for a terrible scolding. She threw abuse at him angrily for not bringing bees' honey. When he protested that drip honey was tastier, she struck him with such force that she knocked out one of his teeth and blood poured down his chest. Maruf hit the side of her face in defence, and tried to hold down her arm, which enraged her all the more.

She managed to seize his beard, and pulled at it hard, screaming at the same time. This brought their neighbours in to see what all the commotion was about. They reproached Fatima sternly for her behaviour, and eventually calmed her down enough for Maruf to be able to sleep the rest of the night in peace.

The next day as soon as he opened the shop, two court officials came for him and took him back to the court house. Maruf was most surprised to see Fatima standing by the judge's side, her elbow bandaged and her veil stained with blood!

The judge chided him, "Are you not ashamed to treat your wife so cruelly?" he said. "You knocked out her tooth and broke her elbow instead of carrying out her simple request."

"As God is my witness," Maruf replied, "I did neither of these things." He then told exactly what had happened from beginning to end.

The judge was a shrewd man and knew how to sum up people. Not only did he believe Maruf's words, but even gave him some money to buy food and to pay the court costs.

The unfortunate cobbler went back to work, but no sooner had he opened his shop, than a man entered with more distressing news.

"Hide, Maruf! The vizier himself has sent his guards to fetch you. Fatima has complained to the Highest Authority!"

What was he to do? The poor cobbler closed the shop hastily, bought some bread and cheese and fled from Fatima and from the city.

He was beyond the city walls when it began to pour with rain. There was no question of going further in such weather. He wandered through some ruins near the walls, hunting desperately for shelter from the torrential rain. At last he found a dark little cell in a crumbling wall where he could lie.

Thoroughly wet and miserable, he gazed unhappily into the growing, rainy darkness, his heart heavy with fear and despair. Where was he to flee to escape from the Ugly Fatima? Tears welled in his eyes and ran down his cheeks. He wept freely and cried to God for help. Suddenly a giant figure rose from the ground in front of him — so black and so terrifying, that it could not have been a creature of this world.

"Why do you weep and disturb my sleep?" the apparition stormed. "I have been living here for two hundred years, and no one from Cairo has dared to disturb me. Now your tears have brought me to you. Your despair fills me with compassion. I wish to help you. Please tell me all that is wrong..."

52

Maruf gaped in astonishment. At the first sight of the monster he thought his last hour had come, but instead he was being offered help! So he poured out all his history and all his troubles, and then told him of his desire to find himself so far away from Fatima that she would never find him.

"Climb upon my back," said the strange genie. No sooner had Maruf obeyed than they were gripped by a mysterious force and flown through the darkness of the night further and further from Cairo. On and on they travelled till the rising of the dawn.

Then their flight slowed down, and soon Maruf felt firm ground under his feet again. They were upon the summit of a mountain, from which they could see clearly a great city surrounded by high walls.

"This is the place where Fatima will never find you," said the genie. "Go down among its people and settle there." And with these words the genie

disappeared. So Maruf descended towards the city gate, still clutching under his arm the bread he had bought in Cairo.

The sun was already high in the sky when he reached the market place, marvelling all along the way at the strange sights and the strange clothes he saw in this very strange city. His dress too drew people's attention, till he was finally stopped by one man, who said, "I can see you are a stranger here. Where are you from?"

"From the city of Cairo," Maruf replied.

"How long have you been travelling?" asked the man.

"Since yesterday," said the cobbler truthfully. But the man, upon hearing this, began to laugh and to call out to people, "Come here, everyone! This man is trying to make me believe that only yesterday he was in Cairo, when we all know that Cairo is a whole year's journey from here!" Everyone crowded around, believing Maruf to be an utter madman. But Maruf showed them his bread and said, "I am not mad! It is you who are being fooled! This bread was baked only yesterday. If any of you have been to Cairo, you must know I speak the truth!"

The people were taken aback — there was no one who could dispute these words or confirm them. Then one man called out, "Let us go to merchant Ali; he comes from Cairo!"

The merchant's house was quite near and once there, Maruf found that in his book of life was written not only misery, but also joy. The merchant first confirmed that the bread really did come from Cairo, and when the crowd had dispersed, he invited the cobbler into his house. There he had him dressed in robes fit for the richest of merchants, offered him delicious foods and wines and asked him for news of Cairo. Eventually he inquired whether Maruf had ever heard of Sheikh Ahmad.

"He was my neighbour when I was a boy," said the cobbler, "and he had a son who was my close friend..."

"He was my father," cried the merchant, and Maruf then realized that the man before him was his long lost companion who had disappeared when only seven years old. It was Ali himself! They embraced joyfully, and then the rich merchant Ali, who had no intention of turning his back on his old friend, offered help and sound advice:

"This city is called Khutan, and it lies so far away from Cairo that no one here can possibly be aware of your work and your poverty. The world is full of idle boasting and lies and asks to be deceived, and this is why I have disguised you as a wealthy merchant. Now I shall lend you a thousand dinars and we shall proceed to the market place where I shall announce that you are one of the world's richest men. When I ask you about your merchandise, you must say that you have an abundance of goods, but that they have been delayed in a caravan. And if a beggar comes to you, give him some alms. All this will make the merchants trust and like you and believe you to be generous. After that it will be easy for you to do business with them. I am confident it will not take long for you to become their equal."

Everything happened as Ali said. Maruf mounted a mule, and a slave walked before him, leading him to the market place. When Ali joined them, they strolled amid the other merchants, Ali pointing from time to time at different goods, saying as he did so, "Tell me, sir, have you brought anything like that material?"

"Yes, of course," Maruf would answer, "yards and yards of it."

Before they reached the far end of the market place, Ali halted and calling together all the merchants, he began to praise the cobbler.

"We must salute and honour the richest merchant of Cairo. We should become his servants, for only so can we do justice to such a noble visitor!"

Maruf, in the meantime, was giving away handfuls of dinars to the poor, so very shortly his purse was emptied.

"You have many poor and needy," he remarked to the nearest merchant. "Had I been aware of this, I would have brought with me at least one saddle bag filled with money, for it is not my custom to ignore the poor... How happy would I be to have at least another thousand pieces of gold, so that I might give them away in alms until the arrival of my own merchandise."

The merchant lent him the thousand dinars, and Maruf continued to give away handfuls of money to the needy. Before that day met night, he had borrowed many times more, till he owed a good fifty thousand dinars.

His friend Ali was watching it all very closely, and was most upset to see Maruf throwing away so much money. He was all the more upset when the cobbler, upon being tackled, replied, "This is nothing in comparison to my caravan! This is such a mean reward..."

What could Ali do now? He could not very well confess the truth, having praised Maruf so highly. He would risk being labelled a liar. Therefore, when a few days later all the creditors complained that Maruf made excuses when asked to repay his debts, he advised, "Put your case to the king, for he too owes me a thousand dinars, and I am loth to ask him for them."

The king of that city was very greedy and when he heard the merchants' laments, he said to himself, "That man would not be so generous if he did not own truly valuable merchandise. I shall have to do my best to gain his trust and friendship before his caravan arrives — for surely I am more worthy of his wealth than those simple merchants... I know what I shall do. He will have my daughter in marriage."

The king hurried to confide his intentions to the vizier. But the vizier had other plans. He intended to wed the king's daughter himself, and so he said, "That man must surely be a liar and an imposter, for he shows no respect for money nor property. If you wish to find out the truth, Your Majesty, you should test him. I know a way which will show him up for what he really is..."

The king thought this very sound advice, so he summoned Maruf to put him to the test.

When the cobbler arrived, he said, "The merchants are complaining that you owe them fifty thousand dinars. Why haven't you settled your debts?"

"Because my caravan has not yet arrived. When it comes, I shall give them double what I have borrowed," was Maruf's reply.

"And what is your opinion of this stone?" asked the king, changing the subject abruptly. And he passed to the cobbler a jewel worth a thousand dinars or more, which he himself particularly treasured.

Maruf held the jewel in his hand, examined it, then pressed it with his fingers till it broke.

"Why did you do that?" cried the astonished king. "Why destroy a jewel worth a thousand dinars?"

"Oh, Your Majesty, I did not dream your treasury was so poor that you value so highly such a little piece of mineral worth a meagre one thousand dinars! In my estimation, the king of a city should have in his possession jewels valued at least seventy thousand dinars each. Such a piece as this is hardly worthy of you."

Hearing such words, the greedy ruler turned greedier still. Such a wealthy merchant as this, he thought, must own a fortune huge enough to fill every inch of his palace.

He therefore forced the vizier to carry on with the wedding arrangements, and ordered the Sheikh el Islam to prepare the marriage contract. Soon the festivities began: the drums were beaten, the city was gaily decorated, the tables were lavishly spread with all kinds of dishes; there were tournaments, performances by clowns and acrobats, and all sorts of

unusual displays. The celebrations continued for forty days and forty nights.

Maruf was overjoyed, for his bride proved to be lovely enough to put the light of the moon to shame. In her honour he asked the king to order the treasurer to fetch gold and silver, so that he could again give freely and generously to the poor and the needy, and to all those who had joined in the festivities. The vizier almost choked with rage to see the king's riches thus squandered.

On the forty-first day a magnificent wedding procession was held and Maruf became husband to the king's daughter.

In the days which followed the happiness of the bride and bridegroom grew, but so did the doubts of the king, for Maruf's caravan still had not appeared. The vizier constantly added fuel to the fire, till the king was so worried and so uneasy that he went with the vizier to his daughter Together they persuaded her to find out the truth about her husband...

Like most women, she was skilled in the gentle art of persuasion. She knew how to coax her husband with words sweeter than honey to tell her anything she wanted to know. Before knowing it Maruf was confessing everything. He told her the full story from beginning to end.

But the loving heart of his wife did not permit such tidings to reach her father's ears.

"I shall never tell him the truth," she vowed. "He would never forgive you, but would slay you, and publicly condemn you as an impostor and a liar. Moreover, he would probably want me to marry someone else, and that I could not bear; I would rather die than consent to that."

"I have a much better idea: I myself will give you fifty thousand dinars and a fast horse. You must disguise yourself, and ride away at once to some foreign land where you can trade as a merchant, enlarge your fortune and return with all respect and honour."

As the night drew to its close they embraced, and Maruf departed from the city, so well disguised that nobody gave him a second glance.

At daybreak the king's daughter visited her father, and said "May God turn his back on your vizier for trying to blacken and dishonour my husband. For only last night ten slaves came to my window, bringing a letter for Maruf which I took and read. It contained bad tidings: two hundred horsemen had attacked Maruf's caravan, stolen two hundred loads of merchandise and killed fifty of his five hundred white slaves. The fight delayed the caravan thirty days. Hearing this news, my husband grew angry, that they had been delayed by such a trivial matter. He decided therefore to join the ten slaves to speed the caravan on. His concern was not for the loss of goods, for compared to his wealth, the two hundred loads are but a grain of sand on the beach!''

This appeased the king yet again, and he scolded the vizier for his suspicious thoughts.

By now Maruf was wandering across the desert track, not noticing nor caring where his horse carried him — for his heart was heavy and pained by the separation from his beloved wife. It was not until noon, as he approached a village, and he saw a ploughman busily tilling his field, that he realized how hungry he was.

The ploughman noticed Maruf's unusual attire and immediately offered to bring him food from the village, and fodder for his horse. Maruf gratefully accepted the offer.

"He left his work on my account," Maruf said to himself, "so I will plough in his stead while he is gone." And bending over the plough he drove the bullocks on. Suddenly the plough struck against something hard in the ground and the beasts stopped. Maruf saw that the plough was caught in a ring of gold which was attached to a large slab of alabaster.

Maruf applied all his strength to lift the boulder from its place. At last it moved, revealing a round opening with stairs which led down into the earth. Maruf did not hesitate, but climbed down. When his eyes grew used to the darkness, they widened with wonder.

He found himself in a spacious underground room with four side alcoves filled from floor to ceiling with the most valuable treasures. The first alcove was filled with gold, the second with pearls, emeralds and corals, the third with jacinths and rubies and turquoises, and the fourth glittered with diamonds and other precious jewels, each one the size of a hazel nut.

Maruf had never seen such riches, indeed, he had never dreamed that they even existed. In the centre of all this wonder stood a chest of clear crystal, and upon that chest was a little gold box. Drawn by a mysterious, magic force he walked over to the box and pushed open the lid. It contained a gold seal ring, the brightness of which almost blinded him.

As he was trying to make out the names and talismans engraved on the ring, Maruf rubbed it to see more clearly... and lo! Out of nowhere a voice behind him thundered, "At your service, master!"

Maruf spun round, but in the darkness all he could see was the outline of a man's body. "Who are you and what are you doing here?" he asked tremulously.

"I am Abussadat, the servant of the seal ring, the bringer of happiness, the executioner of your desires. My power is indeed great. I am the sultan who rules over thousands of genies, and each of those thousands rules over a thousand marids, and each marid has in his power a thousand satans — and every satan is the master of a further thousand genies; all these are under my sway and dare not disobey me. And with all this power I shall now serve you..."

Maruf could scarcely believe his ears.

"What treasures do you guard here? Can you bring them to the earth's surface?" he stammered at last.

"These are the greatest treasures in the world. They were once amassed by the son of Ad before God Almighty's wrath fell upon him for daring to wish to use his power to create a paradise city on earth. But now all this is yours, and we shall take it to the face of the earth!"

With that Abussadat made a sign — and suddenly the underground cavern was filled with movement. Hundreds of handsome young boys appeared and proceeded to carry all the rich chests and baskets of gold and jewels to the earth's surface.

"Who are these boys?" asked Maruf.

"They are my children," was the reply, "and they are honoured to serve you. Now tell me, what else do you demand!"

Maruf then asked for mules to carry the baskets and chests, and Abussadat obliged by transforming half of his children into mules, and the other half into servants and slaves. Then he summoned the marids and turned some of them into horses wearing saddles of gold set with jewels.

When this was done, Maruf had a large luxurious tent pitched for himself, and a whole forest of lesser tents in which all his slaves and attendants could rest and feast before starting the journey to the city of Khutan.

It was just then that the kind-hearted ploughman returned, carrying a large wooden bowl of lentils, and also barley for the horse. His knees grew weak with fear when he saw all the splendour. Thinking that Maruf must surely be the caliph himself, and worrying about the simple meal he had brought him, he was unable to utter a single word.

But Maruf, now richly dressed in royal robes, received the peasant kindly and insisted on eating the simple dish he had brought. He told the peasant to fill his stomach with the exotic dishes on the table, while he, after finishing all the lentils, filled the large wooden bowl with gold. "You were kind to me, so I shall be generous to you," said Maruf, handing over the bowl.

Then he sat down and wrote a letter to the king to inform him he was returning at last with his caravan, and to ask him to come and meet him.

At daybreak the enormous caravan set out — there were seven hundred mules laden with chests and baskets, with slaves and servants and horses and riders all attired in great splendour.

This was the grand spectacle which greeted the eyes of Maruf's father-in-law when the two of them met. And the king, marvelling at Maruf's incredible wealth, rode at his side into the city at the head of this stately procession of riches which would have filled with envy the heart of any king, sultan or caliph.

All the merchants were given back double the amount they had lent. And

as a special gift for Maruf's lovely wife, Abussadat presented her with a robe with pearls and other jewels of priceless beauty.

Everyone was now content and happy — all except the sly vizier, who still hated and envied Maruf.

When an opportune moment came, he remarked to the king, "It all seems very strange, Your Majesty; I cannot see how any merchant can accumulate so many treasures which belonged to royal rulers. And I have never heard of a true merchant throwing away a small fortune to the poor and needy. A real merchant would be aware that he was not only robbing his own pocket, but was also losing a good opportunity to make profit..."

"How do we find out the truth, vizier?" asked the king, showing interest.

"Nothing could be easier. We shall invite your son-in-law into the garden to dine with us and join us in a bottle of wine; and then, when reason flies from his head, we shall get to the real truth."

Soon after this discussion they invited Maruf into the garden as planned, and he, unsuspecting, accepted gladly. When the three of them had dined and washed their hands, the wine was poured into their cups, where it sparkled invitingly. The first sip warmed Maruf's blood, the second turned it into a flame which set his whole body on fire. The king and the vizier only sipped their wine, but urged their companion to drink on and on.

At last the vizier's moment of glory had arrived. Maruf's reason had gone and it was easy to find out all his secrets. Maruf told everything, and even lent the vizier the ring. Thereupon the vizier wasted no time, but rubbed the seal and instantly Abussadat was standing before him.

"I am at your service, master. What is your command?" asked Abussadat, looming above the vizier.

"Take this wretch and put him in the most desolate of deserted lands where he will find no food or water!" the vizier commanded, pointing at Maruf.

As Abussadat seized him and flew off, the vizier turned to the king. "Have I not always said that he was a liar and an impostor?" he asked.

"You were quite right, vizier," the king replied. "Lend me the ring a minute, so that I can have a close look at it..."

The vizier, however, did not hand over the seal ring, but eyed the king angrily, and said, "I am no longer your servant, but your master!" With that he rubbed the seal again and the servant of the ring reappeared.

"What is your command, master?" he asked.

"Take the king and transport him to the side of his son-in-law!" was the order, and though the king pleaded, argued and protested, the servant of the ring dared not disobey. And so Maruf and his father-in-law met again, but this time the meeting was not one of joy and happiness, but of sorrow and despair at being trapped in this most desolate place from which there seemed no hope of escape.

In the meantime the vizier announced to the army and to the city that he was the owner of the magic ring. He threatened that if anyone refused to accept him as the all-powerful new ruler, he would have him also transported to the most desolate place where he would perish of hunger and thirst. That evening he planned to make his innermost dream come true and make the king's daughter his wife.

She, however, already knew about the traitor's intentions, and as she was well acquainted with the magic of Maruf's seal ring, she set a trap for the vizier. Pretending to be very flattered at the purpose of his visit, she turned away at the very moment he was about to embrace her, and said, "This moment should be ours alone, and not shared with an onlooker!"

"Who is here to see us?" asked the vizier, looking around.

"A face is grinning at me from your ring," said the princess.

"But that is Abussadat, my servant!" the vizier replied.

"How dare you permit a servant to look at your future wife?" cried the princess. "Remove that ring immediately!"

The unsuspecting vizier placed the ring upon a cushion, and as he attempted again to embrace her, the king's daughter kicked him with such force, that he fell senseless to the floor. Then she quickly rubbed the ring and said to Abussadat, "Take the vizier to the dungeon and put him in irons. Then hurry to my true husband and to my father! Bring them back immediately!"

What a joyful reunion there was! The king appointed Maruf to the post of vizier in place of the sly traitor, whom he had put to death. The magic ring remained in the possession of his daughter, for she knew better than anyone how to use it wisely. When the king grew old and died, Maruf ruled in his place. And he became the father of a handsome son, who was uncommonly wise.

Life flows by, life ebbs away. The old king's death was followed by an era of contentment and peace for Maruf and his family, which was unhappily interrupted after five years by the illness and then the death of his wife.

Before God took her into his safe keeping, she returned the magic ring to Maruf with the warning, "I beg you to guard it well for your own sake and for the sake of our son, for I fear for you both."

Surely enough, barely two years passed before the hour came when Maruf should have recalled and heeded his wife's words. It was dead of night and he was fast asleep when a sudden movement in his bed disturbed him. He opened his eyes, and thought he must surely be in the land of nightmares — for beside him, on his own pillow lay the head of a hideous old bald-headed hag who was curled like a snake. He recognized her by the large pointed rabbit teeth, and realized he was not dreaming. This was unmistakably ugly Fatima herself — his old wicked wife!

Maruf could easily have had her driven out of the land, for he was now the king and afraid of no one but God himself. Nevertheless he listened with sympathy to Fatima as she told him how, after his departure, she had endured hunger, humiliation and contempt for sinning against him, and how, filled with despair and need, she had run beyond the walls of Cairo, to weep in solitude. There a black genie had suddenly appeared before her, and on hearing of her plight, had carried her to the palace of her former husband.

And she humbled before Maruf as if she were the lowest of slaves. His heart melted and was filled with compassion, and at last he told her she might stay with him.

The very next day he gave Fatima a palace of her own as well as slaves and servants and all the material things she desired. But he himself paid her no attention, remembering all too well how she had ill-treated and persecuted him in the past.

It never occurred to him that she could still harm him in any way, particularly as she kept assuring him of her gratitude.

Yet this would not be the true ugly Fatima if her heart did not again fill with hatred and anger. This time she was fired with jealousy, because Maruf's attentions were centred on a lovely young slave girl. So she decided to destroy him.

Fatima had heard of the magic power of the seal ring, and she found a way of seizing it for her evil purpose. Maruf took the ring off but once a day — when he took his bath before going to bed.

Ugly Fatima chose the blackest of nights for her wicked deed. Unseen, she slipped past the guards into the king's palace and waited in hiding till he entered the bathroom.

64

If night turns a blind eye to evil deeds, it does not turn a blind eye to rightful revenge. It so happened that as Fatima was creeping towards Maruf's bedroom, the seven-year-old prince was awake and so heard her shuffling steps.

He put on his sword and looked into his father's bedroom. The hideous, wicked old hag, whom he always tried to avoid, was searching the room inch by inch, muttering to herself, "Where could he have put that ring?"

The little prince realized immediately which ring she meant. At last she found it and picked it up. The ring was in her hand and she was about to rub it when he sprang towards her, the sword raised above his head. With one swift blow her head was severed from her body.

Maruf, disturbed by the noise, rushed to his son's side. "How often have you asked me, Father," said the boy, "when I would go into battle with my sword? And how often have I replied, that I shall go when the time is ripe, when I shall find a head which deserves cutting down, and when my blow will be the blow of justice? Look, the time has come," he added, pointing to the seal ring clutched tightly in Fatima's hand.

And so Maruf's own son removed the last danger from Maruf's life, and he could live in happiness, comfort and joy for the rest of his days.

Basim the Blacksmith

There are as many tales told of the days of Caliph Haroun al Raschid as there are stars in the night sky; and just as the stars have been shining so long and so far away, these tales have been with us since days of old and have spread far and wide.

It is said that one day the caliph was overcome by moodiness and deep depression, which he tried in vain to dispel. So he summoned his vizier Jafar, and begged for advice. For a while Jafar remained deep in thought, stroking his long beard. At last he pronounced, "We must go to the place where depression and moodiness do not usually visit people's minds. Let us disguise ourselves and go among the simple people. Who knows, something may happen which will cheer your spirits."

Haroun gladly agreed to this proposal. They asked the black hangman Masrur to join them, and the trio set off that night into the silent alleys of Baghdad. They wandered about till the night breeze brought them the distant sound of a merry song:
"How you shine, pearly wine
Kissed by dew, you are mine…"

They rounded a corner and came upon a high house built on stilts; there was a light in the upstairs window, and they could see a shadow with a glass in its hand.

"I am sure to find a remedy for my depression here," said the caliph. "Masrur, get them to open the door and let us in!"

Masrur rapped on the door, and a head as big as a pumpkin peered out of the window and cried, "What do you want, you loafers? Why do you disturb me?"

The caliph could hardly contain his laughter. "We are merchants from distant lands and all we want is to pass a few moments with you, till we feel refreshed and rested!"

The head disappeared, and soon the master of the house loomed in the doorway. He was a real giant of a fellow, who with one swing of his fist could have sent the whole trio to kingdom come.

"You don't look like merchants," he growled. "But very well, come in! Don't think though that I will fuss over you as if you were some gentry! Not a sip, not a bite of food will you get! And you must promise you will never question, or tell to anyone what you will see or hear — now remember, not a single word!"

They entered, half curious, half afraid. Their host was having a feast — the table was laden with meats, fruits and sweets and a large bottle of wine.

They sat down in the manner customary to visitors, but their host was anything but polite. He stuffed himself, he gulped his wine, barking at the same time at Jafar, "Don't get any ideas, you great fat man with the moustache, that you'll have any food from me!"

Next he turned on the black Masrur. "I bet you'd like a drink, and that you'd swallow the lot, you gluttonous devil. You would be like a bottomless jug… But you're not getting one single sip!"

And while he was showering them with abuse and ridicule, the caliph was doubled up with laughter.

It was almost dawn, the dishes were licked clean and the bottle was empty, when Haroun al Raschid asked, "Tell me, sir, who are you that you can dine in such a fine style?"

"Oh, you hypocrites," cried their indignant host. "You're not supposed to ask questions!" Then he added more kindly, "I'll tell you: my name is Basim, and I am a blacksmith. Day in, day out for twenty years now I have been earning five silver dirhams and these buy me a meal which keeps me busy till morning when I return to work. And nothing is going to prevent me from continuing with my usual habits!"

"And what if tomorrow you were to lose your job?" asked the caliph.

"What a poor prophet you are!" roared Basim. "Why should such a thing happen? But if it did, I'd find you, don't you fret, and you would see what I would do to you!"

Haroun laughed and rose. "But we are only passing merchants, so how could we do you harm? The remark was meant only as a joke!"

With that they bade Basim goodbye and they parted. But the abuse and humiliation they had been forced to endure stung and irked the caliph. He was determined to punish the rude blacksmith with the rough tongue. Basim would get his just deserts!

The next morning therefore the caliph said to the commander of the guards, "Starting from now, for the next three days all work in our forges must cease. Whoever disobeys will be shorter by his head!"

Poor Basim! As soon as he heard the news, he thought of the guests he had the previous night. If only he could lay his hands on them!

His head bent, and worrying about his livelihood, he left the forge and turned towards home. He was passing the bath house...

"What is up with you, Basim?" he heard suddenly, and there stood his old friend Calid who worked in the bath house.

The blacksmith told him of his bad fortune, complaining loud and long about his lost living.

"That is easily remedied," said Calid, his hand on Basim's shoulder. "You can work for those three days here with me, and afterwards return to the forge."

And so that day, instead of pounding away with his hammer, he washed customers' feet and rubbed perfumed oils into their skins. Before the time came for afternoon prayers, there were five silver dinars in his hand and he left for home humming merrily. How easy it proved to be a bath house attendant! From now on I shall not earn my living in any other way, he decided.

Night came again, and a round moon sailed above the spires of Baghdad. Once again Basim's window was lit, once again his merry voice was heard. And once again someone hammered on the door.

"I was just thinking about you!" boomed the blacksmith's voice, as he opened the door to the three familiar figures.

But by now the wine had quenched his anger, so he invited the visitors in again, so that he could subject them to further rudeness and abuse.

Haroun al Raschid had only one thought in mind: to discover how Basim had made the money to hold his usual feast.

"You inquisitive fellow!" cried the blacksmith. "I tell you now, your evil prophecy almost came true. But from today, as the caliph ordered all forges to close I am working for good money in the bath house!"

"And what if he closes the bath houses as well?" the caliph could not help asking.

"That would please you, would it not! You are fine fellows to be sure! Out of my house, all three of you!"

It took a long time to calm the blacksmith down. They did not leave his house till just before daybreak.

Haroun al Raschid was agog with impatience to punish the rascally Basim. The moment he was seated in his palace, he commanded that all Baghdad bath houses were to be closed for a period of three days.

This order caused quite a stir among the people, and caused Basim to regret most heartily that he had not kept his mouth closed in front of his night visitors.

But it was no good crying over spilt milk. What was done was done! He would just have to look round for something else to do.

So he went from door to door. But he had no luck, for the rumour that his presence was a bad omen arrived before him. Worn out and dejected, he dragged himself home, and there his glance fell upon a scarf which had been dropped in a corner of his room.

I can sell that for at least five dirhams, thought Basim — and he snatched up the scarf and set off for the market.

On his way he stopped at the medresa, the holy school of Islam, where he went through the customary process of washing himself and praying for the success of his venture. Then he sprinkled holy water on the scarf, and

70

draped it over his turban while he wondered where he could sell it for the highest profit.

As he stood and pondered by the gates of the school of the greatest learning, a woman came to him and said, "Sir, you are a representative of the law, and I have a serious complaint to make!"

She must take me for a law officer, because I am wearing a scarf like they do, the blacksmith rightly guessed. Aloud he said, "What do you want? I shall help you all I can."

"I wish to complain about my cobbler husband. According to our marriage contract I should receive five dinars from him, but so far he has not given me a single penny," sobbed the woman.

"Point him out to me, and I shall make sure he pays up right away," Basim roared in a thunderous voice.

"Shouldn't we first get the order signed by the judge?" the cobbler's wife suggested shyly.

"I myself am authorized to sign all documents," was the reply.

The woman gave Basim two dirhams and said, "Take this for your kindness. My husband is working round this corner."

Basim took the money and flew to the shop. He lifted the astounded cobbler by the scruff of his neck, sat him astride his back, and stretching his long legs to their full length, strode out in the direction opposite to the one where he had left the cobbler's wife. Soon he disappeared from her sight.

"What is going on, sir, where are you taking me?" stammered the frail little cobbler, his knees knocking with fear.

"To the courthouse, of course! You are not paying your wife her dues!"

"Wait, I will explain everything, please stop a moment!" cried the now frantic cobbler, hammering away at the blacksmith's back. At last Basim did stop and put him down.

"What have you to say for yourself then?" he stormed, his eyes rolling threateningly.

"Representative of the law, I promise to pay up and to make peace with my wife, only please don't take me to court..."

"And who is going to pay for my services?" cried Basim.

"Here is something by way of compensation," said the cobbler, offering three dirhams.

"Very well, just this once I'll put in a good word for you," the blacksmith consented, wagging his finger at the cobbler warningly. He accepted the silver coins and dismissed him.

Then he went as usual to buy food and wine for his evening meal. He was looking forward to his evening, for he no longer feared tomorrow. How could the caliph afford to close all the courts? Such an act would cost him dearly! But he would show those three what he was made of!

There was hardly anything left in the bottle by the time they arrived. Perhaps that was why the blacksmith forgot his resolution to keep silent and showered his guests with abuse and insults as usual. And of course, the worse for drink, he let it slip how he had become a representative of the law, and that this was to be his new occupation.

The caliph did not need to know more. The very next morning he called the supreme judge and said to him, "It has come to my attention that among your representatives there are several who have deceived you. They are in their office under false pretences, for their fathers or forefathers have

not been servants of the law. Go and talk to each and every one. Those who have the right to their position are to receive an instant rise in salary, but the impostors are to receive an instant thrashing!''

The high judge was most surprised to hear such words — he could not recall such an order being given ever before. But he hastened to the madrasa, where all the representatives of the law met each morning — Basim amongst them.

In no time at all they were surrounded by guards armed with poles and sticks, while the supreme judge walked round interrogating one after the other. He enquired about their fathers and forefathers, and it did not take long for the blacksmith to realize what was the purpose of these questions and what was in store for him. He knew he could not escape punishment.

Basim was beaten soundly and afterwards the judge chased him out in disgrace, and barred him from the madrasa forever.

The sting of his words was still ringing in Basim's ears as, covered in bruises, he shuffled home. His thoughts were no longer on his daily five dirhams, but on how quickly he could get out of Baghdad.

Once in his house, his eyes wandered round his poor room. There was nothing here to take away but an old sheath which once had held his sword and a club hanging on the wall. With a shrug of his shoulders he tied the sheath to his belt and slid a length of wood into it. But first he cut the top of the stick into the shape of a sword handle. And with the club in his hand — it might come in handy sometimes — he hastened out of the city.

But Basim would not have been Basim if he did not soon become involved in something else. He was passing through the market, so engrossed in his thoughts that perhaps he wasn't even aware where he was. Suddenly he found himself part of a crowd surrounding a pair of men locked in a vicious fight. They were beating and clawing each other, pulling each other's hair and beards, and blood was everywhere. Not one of the onlookers had the courage to interfere.

But when the huge, muscular Basim appeared and raised his club, the fighting ceased instantly.

The complete silence which followed was broken by the voice of the market sheikh, who said, "Thank you, Commander of the Guards, for preserving the peace here. Please accept these five dirhams as a small mark of our respect and gratitude, and take these ruffians to the caliph to get their just deserts!"

"Well, this city must be kindly disposed towards me after all, when I am taken for the caliph's chief guardsman!" Basim said to himself. "I'd be a fool not to give my luck a helping hand!"

So he drove the two men before him to the palace, where he handed them over to the real commander of Haroun's guards.

The strong, muscular figure of Basim and his assured behaviour impressed the guards to such a degree that though they had never seen him before, they accepted him as one of themselves.

"He is sure to be in our master's favour," they remarked amongst themselves, and even the commander trusted him with the most important tasks.

For Basim life was good again. Forgetting his early morning disgrace, he prepared happily for the evening, determined that this time he would send those three merchants packing much the worse for wear.

Haroun al Raschid was also most impatient for darkness to descend over Baghdad. "I wonder if that stupid blacksmith has put two and two together yet?" he thought.

Vizier Jafar and Masrur were not so anxious to pay Basim another visit. "Let us not go there again," they said. "The cup of his patience must surely have overflowed today, particularly as he received a beating he is not likely to forget!"

But the caliph stood firm. "We shall take him five stuffed chickens. That should melt his heart. But first I want to see him miserable and crawling at my feet with his belly rumbling with hunger!"

When night had fallen the three so-called merchants again left the palace through a secret gate and followed the now well-trodden path.

Their destination was still several corners away when they heard their familiar song:

"How you shine, pearly wine..."

They eyed each other questioningly.

"That fellow is incorrigible," muttered Jafar.

"It is therefore all the more important to find out how he came by his earnings," said the caliph and quickened his steps.

The moment they knocked on the door, Basim's head popped out of the window. "Come in, come in, so that I can repay you as you deserve," he cried, brandishing the evil looking club over his head.

"We have come to sit with you for the very last time," said Haroun. "We are leaving the city at dawn, so we wanted you to dine as our guest..."

The blacksmith, seeing and smelling the delicious stuffed roast chickens, could not resist such a temptation.

"In you come then, you rogues, you rascals, you tramps, you parasites!" he snapped in his usual unfriendly way, as he led them up the stairs. "I am not afraid of you now, you scoundrels, whatever you may prophesy! Now I am the servant of our ruler himself!"

The caliph hardly dared breathe, so curious was he. When he discovered how Basim had wormed his way into the midst of his most faithful servants, he began to hatch another plan, paying little attention to what was going on round him.

And the following day he ordered the commander of the guards to send four men to him from his division, the blacksmith among them.

"What does this mean?" Basim wondered. "Is it possible that bad luck is close at my heels here too?"

But what was in store was even worse than he expected.

"My guards," the caliph addressed them, his face hidden behind a handkerchief so that the blacksmith could not recognize him. "It is my command that you do me a service which will prove that you justly deserve the position you hold, and you will be rewarded accordingly. However, if you fail to carry it out, you will lose your heads!"

Haroun al Raschid then gave a sign and four villains were brought forth — four thieving murderers, who already had been sentenced to death by the court.

"It is now up to you to prove your worth. Cut off the heads of these scoundrels with your swords!"

"My last hour has come... The caliph will surely this day cut off my head too," thought Basim, trembling with fear. "How can I behead anyone with a piece of wood?"

Haroun, Jafar and Masrur were holding back their laughter. "Your turn now," said the caliph, turning to Basim, when the other three had completed their tasks and three headless bodies had been carried away.

"Oh, ruler of all believers," cried the blacksmith, falling down on his knees. "Mine is a magic sword inherited from my grandfather, who inherited it from his grandfather. It passes judgement more justly than human wisdom. If it strikes the neck of an innocent man, its blade turns into blunt wood and it springs back. But if the condemned man is truly guilty, it beheads him with one swift blow!"

"Convince us then," said the caliph.

Basim drew out his wooden sword and struck. "Master, this man is innocent, you must let him go!" he cried, backing away as if in fear.

Haroun al Raschid could not contain his laughter any longer. It burst forth like a fountain and he laughed so much the tears rolled down his cheeks and he lay back and laughed till he was exhausted. Then at last he showed his face to the blacksmith.

"I can see, Basim, that nothing is going to suppress your spirit and impudence. I think the best thing I can do is to give up trying and to make you into a real commander of my guards, and also into my dinner companion."

And the caliph, true to his word, fulfilled his promise to Basim.

The Teacher
Who Could not Read

There are some tricksters who outdo all other tricksters, and the ablest of these do not rely so much on their wit as on the trust and faith they build in others. Once they have people's confidence, they find it easy to steer events on the course they choose. For trust can be quite blind, as is proved by the following tale:

As elsewhere in the world, in the land of the Prophet there were cobblers who did not mend shoes, painters who did not paint, merchants who did not barter. In short, these men were the artful dodgers, the tricksters who preferred to devise ways and means to swindle others, rather than live by honest means.

Can you imagine, there was once a teacher who could neither read nor write, and yet he could afford to live in style! This man bought an oversized turban and many charts and tablets covered with letters and sums. He displayed them for all the world to see in a prominent place, so no passer-by could fail to notice them. He himself sat by the school door puffing at his pipe.

People who passed by were impressed, and remarked, "This must indeed be a good teacher. Look at all those charts and tablets! We must send our children to him!"

Very soon his school was full and he had to start teaching. How did he manage it? I will tell you: he distributed the charts amongst the children to copy and read. One cannot say it worked very well, but some of the clever children learned to do sums on their own, or from pupils from other schools; others learned to read, and so they taught each other.

And all the time the teacher remained by the front entrance puffing at his pipe. Only when the class was really noisy did he rouse himself to control his pupils with his cane. Believe it or not, the children progressed to the satisfaction of their parents, who held the trickster in their highest esteem, taking him for a wise and learned man.

But one day he was almost caught out:

He was sitting in his usual place when he noticed a countrywoman approaching with a sheet of paper in her hand.

"I'm sure it is a letter she wants me to read," he thought, and he tried to slip out of sight. But alas, it was too late, for there she was, right in front of him.

"My husband sent me this letter; read it to me, please," she asked him, handing the sheet over.

There was no way out. He turned the paper to the left, to the right, upside down and back to front, his brow creased in a frown, his face serious, muttering under his breath.

The woman could hardly bear him to speak. "My husband isn't ill? Not worse news, I hope... Surely he isn't dying... or dead?" she whispered, close to tears.

The man eyed her gravely, nodded his head, raised his index finger and sighed deeply.

"Should I then tear my robe and beat my brow?" cried the woman.

80

"Fate demands it!" replied the schoolteacher, giving her back the letter. With that he turned and entered the school, his head held high.

The countrywoman fell to her knees, ripped her robe and beat her brow. She wept all the way home and all the villagers rushed to her side to see what ailed her.

"Alas, my husband is dead, that is what is written here," she sobbed showing everyone the letter.

One of her neighbours suddenly appeared at her side and cried, "Stop your tears, for your husband is anything but dead! In fact he is as healthy as you or I! All his letter says is that he is sending you a new blanket in which he has wrapped presents for you. Why, I happened to be with him when he was writing!"

"What is this? And to think I grieved for nothing, and tore a good dress to ribbons for nothing," cried the furious woman. Turning on her heel, she raced like a fury back to the schoolhouse.

She found the teacher in his usual place.

"What lies you told me! I have just found out that it states here that my husband is sending me a blanket wrapped round presents!" she shouted, waving the letter before his eyes.

The teacher, however, was not in the least put out. Far from admitting the truth, he shouted back, "That is exactly what I told you, but you went on about him dying or being dead! And as a blanket with parcels in it resembles a shroud with a body in it, you confused me. I vow I shall never bother to read letters again to fools such as you!" he added, turning away from her indignantly.

What could the poor woman do? She apologized again and again to this rascally teacher, till at last he accepted her apologies and pretended to forgive her.

And so the children of that school had to continue to learn by themselves, and the teacher, until the day he died, did not even know how to sign his own name.

The Serpent Queen

In the ancient days of wise men there lived a scholar called Daniel. For many years he longed for a son. When at last his wish was about to be realized, he was alas already old and dying.

Before he died, he summoned his wife to his bedside and bade her farewell with the words, "I must leave you, and I know that when I am gone, my son shall be born. He is sure to ask one day what inheritance his father has left him. I am therefore bequeathing him the chance to gather all the knowledge and wisdom he can learn."

Hasib was born soon after the scholar's death. His mother wanted him to have the best upbringing and the best education, so she sent him to school when he was five years old.

But Hasib was not like his scholarly father. At school he did not bother to learn; he was not even fit to take up a trade. It seemed that Daniel's son was a true idler, not interested in any work, satisfied with loafing about. His poor mother was at her wits' end. What was she to do with him? In the end some neighbouring woodcutters took pity on her and took her lazy son into the forest to work with them.

To everyone's surprise Hasib did not remain idle, but helped to chop wood and transport it, and the woodcutters had no complaints. One day it started to pour with rain. They all took shelter in a cave and waited for the rain to stop.

Hasib sat slightly apart from the others, and amused himself by striking his axe against the boulders under his feet. Suddenly he heard a hollow sound, which told him there must be a space underground. He loosened the boulders and pulled them aside. There, right below him gaped a black opening, out of which oozed the strong aroma of bees' honey. His cries brought the other woodcutters to his side. One of them put his hand inside the opening. As soon as he felt the rich, sticky substance with his fingers, there were no more doubts — Hasib had discovered a huge basin of honey.

The woodcutters knew immediately how to profit from such a valuable find. They ran home to fetch jugs, pans, any vessels they could find. While Hasib guarded the cave, they sold the honey in town till the basin ran dry.

In just a few days they turned into wealthy merchants. But as the supply of honey grew less, they were faced with the problem of rewarding Hasib — for after all, he was the one who had found the honey and so had the right to the largest share of the profit!

"There is only one thing to do. We'll have to get rid of him," the eldest woodcutter pronounced after much thought. All the others readily agreed, for now that they had become rich, they had also become greedy and miserly.

So they decided on a plan. They lowered Hasib into the basin on a rope to collect the very last remains of honey, and when his feet touched the ground, they threw the rope after him. They then blocked the opening with the heavy boulders and ran back into town, crying that the poor unfortunate Hasib had been torn to pieces by wolves.

And while his mother was weeping and grieving for her only son, he was sitting at the bottom of the deep basin wondering how he could escape.

His eyes suddenly noticed a spot where the jet black darkness was slightly broken by a faint, narrow flicker of light. He crawled closer, groping with his hands round the walls of the underground cave. There was a place where the wall was loose and gave away slightly under the pressure of his fingers. Hasib's hands became raw and bleeding as he frantically worked trying to enlarge the opening, but the streak of light widened.

At last the opening was large enough to squeeze through. He found himself in a well-lit, winding passage which took him to a black iron gate behind which gleamed a silver door with a gold key in the lock. He turned the key and opened the door. And there before him was a dazzling green lake, so bright, he had to turn his gaze away.

But this was no ordinary lake. Instead of water, the green surface sparkled with emeralds, which held in their centre a raised gold throne surrounded by hundreds of little seats. Hasib started to count them, but as

84

he was very tired, his head began to nod and soon he was fast asleep.

Who knows how long he slept! He was awakened by a strange hissing sound, as if he were surrounded by thousands of serpents. There were not only thousands, but tens of thousands massed round him as far as the eye could see. They sat on the little seats, their bodies swaying from side to side, their angry black eyes fixed upon him.

On the royal throne sat a serpent with the face of a beautiful maiden. She spoke with a human voice. "Do not fear, Hasib, I know you are my destiny. While you stay here, no harm will come to you. I am the serpent queen, and I was fated to teach you wisdom. Not until you are wise and knowledgeable will you be able to return to your people..."

Hasib was not sure whether he was awake or dreaming, but when the queen gave the order for fruits and nuts to be brought, he became a little bolder. Once he had eaten, he told her all that had happened to him.

"You have no knowledge of the world yet," said the serpent queen, when he had finished. "Now I shall talk and you will listen, and I will not stop till your head is filled with learning and wisdom and till you begin to miss the world..."

Days flew by, nights flew by, and all that time Hasib was discovering and learning all the worldly wisdom. Two whole years passed before he even remembered his home. But then he began more and more to feel homesick, till at last he confided his desire to leave the realm of the serpent queen.

"I knew you would want to return home one day, and I cannot prevent you from doing so. There is only one thing you must promise me, for my life depends on it. You are never to enter a bath house, you are never to allow anyone to lay their eyes upon your naked body..."

Hasib could not understand such a strange request, but he gladly agreed.

The queen showered him with gifts from her wealth of treasures and then led him through winding passages to the earth's surface. Hasib hastened home as fast as he could, and how overjoyed his mother was to see him alive and well after two whole years!

Even the former woodcutters, who now were wealthy merchants, welcomed his return. Every one of them gave Hasib half of his property, so Hasib too soon became a highly respected man.

Now at last his neighbours recognized him as the scholar Daniel's own true son. For now he was able to discuss any subject with confidence and authority, and there was no branch of learning that was beyond his intelligence.

It was natural therefore that Hasib became a frequent guest at the sultan's court. Here too everyone marvelled at his vast knowledge, and only the vizier Shumhur secretly envied him.

But one sad day Sultan Karazdan became ill with the gravest disease — leprosy, and no one, not even Hasib, knew how to help him.

It so happened that the vizier Shumhur one day invited Hasib to his bath house. Hasib hesitated, but the vizier would not take no for an answer. Once he was stripped of all his clothes and stood there naked, the vizier, seeing his body, called forth his guards.

"Do you still insist that you do not know a remedy for the sultan's illness?" he asked, and added, "Look at your stomach, it is black! Only those who are acquainted with the serpent queen have a black stomach!"

"What has that to do with the sultan's illness?" asked the perplexed Hasib, and the vizier went on to explain.

"I see you still do not have quite all the wisdom which lies in books, for it is written down that the only remedy for leprosy is the cooked flesh of the serpent queen. And as you are the only person who knows where she resides, you must lead us to her hiding place. Otherwise the sultan will die and you likewise will die."

The reluctant Hasib had no choice but to agree, and he led the vizier and his soldiers to the cave. There was no need for him to search for the underground passage; the serpent queen was already waiting.

"I know why you have come, Hasib," she said in greeting. "I also know that I must die, though I tried to prevent it and to alter my destiny. Do not fear for me, but take me to the sultan's palace."

To the soldiers' astonishment Hasib gathered the serpent queen in his arms and carried out her request.

Once in the palace the vizier hurried to the sultan to inform him of the good tidings. Hasib and the serpent queen remained for the moment alone.

"Listen well to the last words I am about to utter," said the serpent queen. "Vizier Shumhur desires your death. When I am slain, he will chop my body into little pieces and put them to cook in a pan. He will ask you to skim the froth which will form on top and put in into a bottle.

"Do as he asks, but keep your eye on that bottle, for soon afterwards the

froth will start rising again from the pan, and the vizier will hand you an identical bottle to fill. Do not drink from that second bottle!''

Before the serpent queen had finished speaking, the vizier came back, a sharp knife in his hand, and Hasib heard no more.

Everything happened exactly as she had said. When the time came for the cooked flesh of the serpent queen to be passed to the sick sultan, the vizier said, "Give me the first bottle of froth and you shall open the second one. We shall drink from them together and we shall become the wisest of all the wise men..."

Hasib remembered the warning of the unfortunate serpent queen, and he handed the second bottle to the unsuspecting vizier. The moment Shumhur swallowed the first dose, his eyes turned to heaven and he fell back dead — perishing by the very means he had prepared for the man he envied.

Once Sultan Karazdan had eaten the serpent's flesh, his health gradually improved, till he was completely cured. The grateful ruler made Hasib the supreme vizier of his land. It was a wise act, for who in all the land had more knowledge and wisdom in his head than Hasib, who had been taught by the serpent queen herself?

Hasan the Goldsmith

Nobody remembers now when it happened; it was so long ago. But one thing is certain: in those ancient times a young goldsmith named Hasan lived in Basra, and though he was not exactly prosperous, he was very popular on account of his pleasant and handsome appearance, and his kind, likeable nature.

Now while the goldsmith sat in his shop one day after the afternoon prayers, a stranger entered. By his attire he was a Persian and on his head he wore a large scarlet turban. Though he had never met Hasan, he showered him with compliments, praising his work and his handsome looks in a voice as sweet as honey.

"I do not have a son, Hasan," he confided with a sigh, "and I should like to look upon you as if you were my own boy, for in this short time I have grown most fond of you. To prove I am sincere and serious, I am going to chase poverty from your door forever, by teaching you the secret art of making pure gold out of ordinary copper."

Young Hasan dared not believe his own ears, but the stranger continued, "I shall convince you. Light the charcoal and melt some copper. Then you will see for yourself!"

Hasan obeyed. He cut an old copper plate into small pieces and threw them into the crucible and blew upon it with the bellows till the pieces turned to liquid. Then the Persian took a small paper bag from his turban and sprinkled some of the yellow powder it contained into the melted copper. Red smoke rose from the crucible and the stranger said, "When the smoke evaporates, you will be convinced of the truth of my words."

And truly — there was a lump of gold gleaming in the crucible! When Hasan saw this, he was so astounded he could barely stammer out words of thanks. But the Persian interrupted, "Now you can see I mean what I say. But to become wealthy it needs more than one lump of gold. We have to find much more of the magic ingredient to add to the copper. I know how to prepare it — it is made from herbs which grow at the very top of Cloud Mountain. If you agree, we will go there."

Of course Hasan wanted to go! He could hardly wait. Visions of wealth had clouded his senses and reason, so he replied without hesitation, "I am ready now. I have no idea where this Cloud Mountain lies, but I am confident you will lead me to it."

"The Cloud Mountain lies on a distant island in the middle of the sea," whispered the Persian, as if he feared that he might be overheard. "My boat is anchored in the harbour; we can sail forth today. The magic herbs are in full bloom just now."

That was all the young goldsmith needed to hear. Hurriedly he locked up the shop, and long before the stars brightened the night sky, they were sailing across the wide sea.

The next day came and went, and the second, and the third... The sun rose and set many more times before the morning came when the ship quickened her speed and the sky darkened with strange black clouds.

"We are nearing our destination," the Persian said to Hasan. And truly it was so. A black speck appeared in the sea, and the nearer they came, the larger it grew, and soon they could make out the outline of a mountain rising from the sea. It was well named Cloud Mountain, for its summit was lost in the clouds.

They anchored by the shore.

"How can we reach the summit?" Hasan asked, gazing at the sheer impassable mountain walls.

"I have thought of that," said the Persian, and out of his bag he took a golden drum and a pair of golden drumsticks. He proceeded to beat the drum, whereupon three camels appeared, attracted by the sound. The Persian slaughtered them all and stripped one of its skin. He then sewed the skin up again, leaving a small opening underneath.

"Now listen well, Hasan," he said. "You are to crawl into this skin and wait for the vultures to come and carry you off to the summit. As soon as they fly out of sight again, cut yourself free, climb out and gather the herbs you will see around you."

"How am I to get back?" asked Hasan anxiously.

"Don't worry, I will help you down, but now you must hurry and hide in the skin. And remember, you must only pick the plants which are in flower!"

Hasan thereupon entered the skin — and he was just in time too. Piercing cries were already echoing from the clouds as three enormous vultures dived down. In the twinkling of an eye each one seized a dead camel and rose into the clouds. Smiling with satisfaction under his scarlet turban, the Persian watched their flight until they disappeared from view.

Some time later Hasan felt himself being put down. He was on firm ground again. He peered out from inside the skin, and seeing nothing of the vultures, he widened the opening and crawled out.

He was on the peak of Cloud Mountain. All around him grew herbs with golden flowers and many old human bones lay among them. Hasan did not let that worry him. He picked the magic herbs till there was not a single plant left. Then he walked over to the edge of the steep cliff and shouted down, "I have them all ready. What do you want me to do now?"

"Tie them into a bundle, and throw them down to me," the Persian's voice called from a great distance.

Hasan did as he was told, tied the herbs in a big bundle and threw them over the top.

"What now, sir? How do I get down?" he cried.

"You will never come down again, you fool, unless you want to throw yourself down to a certain death! I am leaving you up there for the vultures to tear you apart, and for the sun to bleach your bones as it bleached the bones of all those who came before you!" cried the Persian, laughing wickedly.

"What about our friendship? You said that you think of me as your own son... You cannot forsake me! You cannot leave me here alone!" Hasan protested, almost in tears.

"What would I want with your friendship? I am Bahran, the follower of Fire and the greatest enemy of all Muslims," cried the voice from below. "Surely you do not think I would have told you the secret formula if I could have obtained the herbs myself! I curse you and all your generation in the name of Fire!" the Persian added, his voice full of hate. Then he picked up the bundle of herbs and walked off calmly towards his ship.

Hasan was speechless with fright. So that was it then! His reward for helping Bahran was to be left at the mercy of the wild, merciless vultures...

I would rather perish by leaping into the sea than wait to be torn apart by them, he thought. Sadly he recited a passage from the Koran, begging God for his deliverance — for only the will of the Almighty determines our destiny — and then he plunged from the summit of Cloud Mountain into the foaming, turbulent sea.

He lost consciousness as he fell, but it must have been the will of Allah that he did not die. He woke to find himself being carried by the waves to safety on a great rock. Carved out of this rock a staircase wound upwards. Hasan climbed to the top and found to his amazement a palace built entirely of gold!

Hasan had to protect his eyes, so fierce was the dazzling glare of the whole building. Nevertheless he took courage and walked through the gates. He came upon two damsels sitting on the terrace playing chess. They were as beautiful as the face of the moon — more beautiful than anything and anyone Hasan had ever seen. He stopped hesitatingly before them, bowing his head in greeting. The youngest one called, "You must be Hasan the blacksmith, whom Bahran brought here this year! Come and tell us how you escaped from his clutches!"

They know me, thought the bewildered Hasan, and he told the maidens everything that had happened to him from first to last.

"Oh, that wicked scoundrel!" cried the older girl, when he had finished.

"We have been living on this side of Cloud Mountain for as long as we can remember, and we do not have much idea what happens on the farther side. You see, our father is the king of the genies, and he gave this palace to me and to my sisters, for he considers this to be the safest place in the world. We have heard that Bahran comes here once a year, always in the company of a different youth, but we never dreamed what an evil fate he prepares for them. Now that we know, and with your help, we will repay him in full!"

"Until then you must stay and be our companion," added the younger girl merrily, and Hasan gladly agreed.

He discovered there were altogether six beautiful daughters of the king of the genies living in the palace, and that each day they took their turn to hunt and to cook. For Hasan they chose a private chamber whose richness and elegance matched their own, and they treated him as a true brother. It was therefore not surprising that he did not miss the outside world.

Time sped by as fast as the running tide, and before he realized it, a whole year had passed. The very morning Bahran was once again due to sail to Cloud Mountain, the eldest princess said to Hasan, "The time for revenge is here, and your weapons are ready!"

She signalled with her hand, and the servants brought Hasan a saddled horse of the finest breed, dressed him in an officer's attire and armed him with a sharp sword. Then they all rode out through the gates.

The ship lay already anchored by the shore. As they drew near, Bahran was in the act of forcing a frightened young Muslim to crawl into the camel skin.

"Stop!" Hasan cried, riding like the wind to their side. "Or you will be struck down by an awful fate."

At seeing him alive, Bahran's knees started to shake, so terrified was he. By then the young goldsmith was looming over him.

"I can see that you have not given up your evil practices, so I have come to settle the score!" Hasan stormed, and before the wretched Bahran had a chance to defend himself, he was shorter by his head.

Hasan took the drum and the drumsticks from him and turned to the young Muslim, who was eyeing him with awe. "Board the ship and sail for home, for nothing but destruction awaited you here."

The ship was soon lost from sight, and Hasan returned with the princesses to the golden palace, where they all continued to enjoy life to the full.

But it was written in the book of destiny that a day would come which would completely alter the course of Hasan's life. It happened that the princesses were invited by their father, the king of the genies, to attend the

wedding of one of their royal relatives. Because of Hasan, the damsels would have preferred to remain in their golden palace, but they had to respect their father's wish.

"Be of good cheer," they said to comfort him. "Our house is your house. You are our brother now. You can make merry, you can hunt and feast and read whilst we are gone, and the time will pass quickly till our return."

They were to be absent for more than two months. When they bade him farewell, the eldest princess handed him the keys to all their rooms and said, pointing to one particular key, "This key opens the door of a chamber which you must not enter. Pay attention to this warning, if you want peace to remain in your heart..."

Hasan asked no questions. He was too saddened by the thought that he was to be separated from his dear sisters. Heavy-hearted, he watched them ride away from the palace.

Now that he was alone, Hasan passed the time hunting and eating and reading. As the days went slowly by, boredom and loneliness made him dispirited and gloomy, and he took to wandering about the empty palace passages and luxurious chambers, examining and admiring their elegance. But he became obsessed with the thought of opening the forbidden door. Though he hesitated for some days, in the end curiosity overcame him. He turned the key and pushed open the door.

There was no luxurious chamber here — just a bare room with a flight of stairs at the far end. These stairs, however, were thickly carpeted and the walls above them were studded with jewels. Hasan hesitated only a moment, gathered his courage and then he climbed the stairs. They led him into a maze of passages and chambers, which eventually opened out on the roof of the palace. There beneath him lay green fields and beautiful gardens full of wild beasts and birds, and beyond was the roaring, foaming sea. Hasan walked on till he came upon a sparkling green pool bordered by magnificent, scented flowers, shrubs and trellises adorned with bars of gleaming gold and emeralds and pearls, each the size of a pigeon's egg.

"Not even the most powerful of all rulers possesses such wealth," Hasan marvelled in amazement at what he saw. And he sat down under a hedge to enjoy all the perfection round him.

He was out of sight just in time, for at that very moment there was a sudden rustle of wings and a large and beautiful white bird flew from the skies onto the soft green lawn. It looked around carefully, but did not see the young intruder who was hidden by the branches.

To Hasan's surprise the bird began to peck the feathers on its chest and to tear them apart with its talons. The skin suddenly split open and a damsel stepped out, whose loveliness almost took Hasan's breath away. Her mouth had the beauty of Solaiman's with lips like coral, her cheeks were like anemones, her eyes like the eyes of a gazelle; her hair was blacker than the darkest night, and when her face broke into a smile, her teeth were as dazzling as pearls strung on a necklace of gold.

Hasan could not tear his eyes away from this vision of loveliness and he felt waves of joy and love flooding his heart. Too late he knew now why the princesses had not wished him to pass through the forbidden door, for he felt quite overcome with love for this beauty.

At long last he forced his gaze away and in a trance retraced his steps to the palace. He must try not to give his secret away! He must not let anyone know where he had been!

But he could not sleep, or eat, or drink, or rest. He could only weep and pine and long for the beautiful damsel, who had set his heart on fire with love.

And then the two months had passed and a cloud of dust in the distance announced the princesses' return. There was hustle and bustle by the palace gates and soon Hasan could hear the six familiar voices calling his name.

They were shocked to see his changed appearance — so thin, so pale, so weak. But he pretended nothing was amiss, and listened with a forced smile to their chatter about the journey and their stay.

He made himself join in the conversation, but his heart was not with them, and his usual happy nature was gone. As days passed he grew so frail from desire to see again the unknown damsel that he became too ill to leave his bed.

Perhaps he would have died of sorrow, if it had not been for the youngest princess — the one he loved best. She spent endless hours at his bedside, caring for him, fearing for him, pleading to know what was wrong, till in a moment of weakness he confided in her.

"You poor unfortunate man!" she cried, when she heard his secret. "Why, that was our beautiful sister Manarassanah, who must never be seen by a human eye! Not even we — her sisters — can ever speak to her. It is the will of our father, the king of the genies. You must forget her, for your love can lead only to sorrow..."

"Alas, dear sister, it is too late, I cannot forget her. I am so consumed with love that if I cannot win Manarassanah for my wife, I shall die," Hasan replied, despair in his voice, tears in his eyes.

What could the princess do? In vain she tried to comfort and cheer him. The youth she had chosen as a brother was growing weaker with each hour, wasting and withering like a fine fresh sprig dries out and withers in the merciless heat of the desert. In the end the youngest sister told the others and persuaded them to agree that in spite of the danger, they would help their brother.

One morning they came to his bedside and the youngest princess said, "We cannot permit our own brother to perish, though we shall not escape punishment and shall probably never see you again. But you must remember my words, Hasan. When you come to the pool and Manarassanah throws her feathered dress aside, take her hand and do not allow her to touch even lightly the plumage. Otherwise she will be back in the powers of the king of the genies and you will never meet her again."

On hearing these encouraging words, Hasan came to life again. He rose from his bed and hastened through the forbidden door...

Everything went well and a little later he returned with the smiling Manarassanah. Her face told of her own love for the kind and handsome youth.

The princesses made preparations for their wedding, and by the following day the golden palace was buzzing with activity, merriment, singing and dancing in honour of Hasan and his bride. Hasan joined in as in a dream, for such magnificent celebrations were unheard of even at the sultan's court!

When after forty days and forty nights the festivities ended, Hasan knew the time had come for him to leave Cloud Mountain with his bride. He was homesick and it was not safe to prolong their stay, for the king of the genies was expected to arrive any day.

The princesses gave them many fine gifts of gold and jewels which were put into large chests. When all was ready for their departure, Hasan beat the golden drum and three camels appeared. He sat on one, Manarassanah on the second, and the third was laden with the chests. As they were about to leave, the youngest sister, unobserved by anyone else, handed a sealed package to Hasan, and whispered, "This bag contains Manarassanah's dress of bird feathers. You must not destroy them, but as long as you hold them in your possession, she will be yours. Hide them well, for she must never find them, or you will lose her to our father again..."

The princesses were loth to see Hasan go — they had grown to love him even more as their own true brother. So they all wept as Hasan left with his bride — the youngest of them most of all.

Once home, Hasan reopened his business. But it was no longer a poor little shop, but a large, imposing place with many workrooms and sales rooms which soon became renowned far and wide. All the rich gentry, wealthy merchants and the viziers were his important and frequent customers, and more than once he was honoured by an order from the sultan himself.

Hasan lived happily with Manarassanah and it seemed that nothing could mar their joy. But, alas, when the thought of harm or evil could not have been further from their minds, disaster struck.

The young goldsmith had to go away for several days on business, and Manarassanah remained at home alone. Out of boredom and curiosity she began to go through all the rooms and halls of their house, till at last she entered the chamber where her husband had hidden the sealed bag containing her feathered dress. Eventually she came upon the package and broke the seal. As soon as her eyes rested on the feathers, she was filled with an unexplainable, irresistible urge to turn into a bird once more. She hesitated for a moment — for it seemed as if an inner voice was warning her against it. Then she shrugged her shoulders and thought: "I'll only try it on again, and then put it back in its place, and no one shall be the wiser."

She put on the feathered dress and turned into the white bird. Then a strange, invisible force seemed to draw her towards the open window. The wings opened of their own accord, and Manarassanah found herself flying high above her house. Alas, too late, she realized that she was back in the power of the king of the genies. Now she knew it was his will which was compelling her to fly far, far away to his residence, to the distant Island of Wak.

Hasan, now on his way home, heard the plaintive cries of his wife far above him. Baffled, he gazed up into the skies, where the sound seemed to come from. He saw the beautiful white bird, he heard Manarassanah's final despairing words, "You will find me on the Island of Wak! The Island of Wak..."

Nothing but a small white speck remained in the sky now... and soon that too was gone...

Hasan realized immediately what must have happened during his absence. He groaned with the pain which pierced his heart, and covering his face with his hands, wept bitter tears. What hope was there that he would ever see his beloved Manarassanah again?

But as the day passed by in mourning and weeping for his lost wife, it occurred to him that there was one place where he might find help. He must go immediately to seek his sisters on Cloud Mountain. The thought comforted him, and he decided to leave at once. He closed his shop, beat the golden drum, and in a trice the three camels were flying across the desert like shadows chasing sunbeams.

They did not stop till they came to the golden palace. The moment the princesses saw Hasan, they rushed through the gates to greet him.

"What brings you here, dear brother?" asked the youngest one. "You must know that when you led Manarassanah from here, the king of genies turned into your enemy — so this territory is dangerous for you!"

"Your father has my beloved wife back in his possession as he always wanted," Hasan whispered, and sighed. And he told them all that had happened. "I am here to beg for your help," he added. "Where is the Island of Wak and how can I reach it?"

The princesses looked embarrassed and remained silent. At last the eldest one spoke. "The journey to the Island of Wak lasts seven human lives; not even your fastest camels can shorten it!"

"That is because your journey will be strewn with seven times seven mortal dangers, which an ordinary human being cannot avoid," explained another sister.

"It is said that only the person who has the magic cap and magic rod can survive the trip," interrupted the youngest princess. "These two things have more power than the all powerful king of the genies! But all we know is that they belong to a wicked magician, and that he has hidden them in a cave..."

"I shall find the magic cap and rod, and I shall set Manarassanah free. Where can I find the magician?" Hasan cried out impatiently.

The answer did not please him.

"We do not know, dearest brother, his whereabouts, for whoever puts the cap on his head, becomes invisible, and with the aid of the rod he can go anywhere he desires..."

"If it is necessary and that is my destiny, I shall search for the magician till the end of my days," Hasan announced.

In this he stood firm. He left soon afterwards, and as the golden palace disappeared before him, he was carried by the three camels across the

parched desert, over mountains and valleys and seas. Hasan did not know
how many nights passed before he came to a small island in the middle of
a vast ocean. There was not a living soul in sight, and at first it seemed the
island was uninhabited. He noticed at the foot of a rocky slope an opening
into a cave, and went to investigate. As he approached, he heard
quarrelsome voices of two boys. "Mine is the cap and yours is the rod!"

"No, I want the cap! Come outside and let's settle this once and for all!"

Before Hasan realized what was happening, the lads appeared, the long
searched for cap and rod in their hands. "You decide, stranger," said the
bigger boy. "Our father was a mighty magician and when he died, he left

us this cap and this rod. But we are not sure which one belongs to whom."

"I will be the judge," Hasan agreed at once. "Go and find a pair of stones of identical size; whoever throws his stone the furthest will get the cap. While you are looking, I shall hold on to both cap and rod."

"That seems very fair," said the boys enthusiastically and ran off to the beach to find the stones.

The moment they were gone, Hasan put the cap on his head and said to the rod, "Take me to the Island of Wak!"

The earth rumbled and trembled, and four spirits as black as coal swished through the air to his side. They seized the young goldsmith by his hands and feet and flew off as swiftly as an arrow to the island of the king of the genies, while on the ground below the two sons of the magician gaped after them in astonishment.

Hasan was so afraid the spirits might let him drop that he kept his eyes tightly shut all the way. Not until the flight was over and he felt firm ground under his feet did he dare open his eyes and examine his surroundings.

He was on the Island of Wak. All around him there were genies, marids and other spirits running to and fro, but no one of them paid him any attention. "This must be because I have the cap on my head and I am invisible," Hasan thought. So unseen and confident, he began his search for Manarassanah.

He traversed the whole island, he searched every corner of every house, the markets, the gardens, even the barracks of the guards. There was not an inch left unsearched, except for the royal palace. But in the palace too there was no sign of his beloved wife. He was just about to give up in despair when fortune smiled on him at last. He was standing by the heavy iron gates which led into the underground prison when he overheard the conversation of two guards. One was telling his companion that the king kept his daughter, Manarassanah, in the deepest dungeon, so that he, Hasan, would never find her.

Hasan's first impulse was to rush into the dungeon. But he decided that it would be wiser to wait till nightfall when everyone was asleep and no one would discover till morning that he had carried off the princess.

He curbed his impatience and waited. At last night came and Hasan, the cap on his head, slipped silently through the maze of dark, winding passages and low damp stairways till he came to the dungeons. The dampness and the gloom depressed him. Would he ever find his beloved wife? He seemed to have been searching and groping in the blackness for so long without success. But then at last he came to a door. Behind it lay the sleeping princess!

How his heart raced, how it pulsed with joy! Taking the cap off his head, he lightly stroked the girl's pale cheek.

"Hasan!" she cried, and fainted with sheer happiness at seeing her beloved. Hasan wasted no time. He had heard a sound on the stairway behind them. Quickly he said to the rod, "Take us to the golden palace on Cloud Mountain!"

And once again the rod did not fail him. A swarm of little spirits dived to their side and in a trice they were both being lifted out of the dungeon, out of the prison, and carried swiftly through the paling night.

When Hasan dared at last to glance over his shoulder, he was dismayed at what he saw. The king of the genies was in close pursuit, riding like the wind in a gold coach drawn by a team of marids. He was so near, in fact, that Hasan could see his face — and his angry, threatening expression terrified him.

"Bring fog and mist down upon our pursuer!" Hasan commanded the rod, and immediately all behind them was enveloped in a thick white blanket.

Below land and sea came into view alternately. Manarassanah opened her eyes and huddled close to Hasan for protection. As she opened her lips to speak, an angry voice roared from behind, "You will not escape me! You belong to me."

The king of the genies was again close behind.

"Let the rain pour down behind us!" Hasan cried, and a torrent of water slowed down the gold carriage for the second time.

Now they could see before them the familiar outline of Cloud Mountain, and on it a speck which shone like the glittering sun — the golden palace!

But the king of the genies was approaching closer yet again... "I have you!" he cried, rising in his carriage, his sword ready to strike.

But Hasan once more shouted to the rod, "Bring thunder and lightning!"

A fiery arrow sliced the sky in half, and with a tremendous crash it shattered the gold coach into a thousand pieces.

Hasan and Manarassanah were now standing in the palace forecourt, and the six sister princesses were running towards them. But before they could embrace, their father, the king of the genies stood before them. His turban was as high as the tallest turret and his thick white beard flowed to the ground.

"Are you not aware that you cannot escape the king of the genies and that I shall punish you, no matter who you are?" he stormed at Hasan.

"I do not fear you, for you accuse me unjustly," Hasan bravely replied. "I too have magic to help me. With this cap and the rod I can escape from you always. But that is not so important. The only thing that matters to me is the love of your daughter Manarassanah, who is mine according to our proper marriage contract. Oh king of kings", Hasan humbly continued, "I shall gladly give you the rod and the cap to win your favour and heart."

The old king's wrath was dying.

"If it is as you say, I shall accept your offer. Give me the rod and cap..."

Hasan passed him both the cap and rod without hesitation. But the king of the genies unsheathed his sword, and brandishing it above his head, he cried menacingly, "Now you are defenceless, I am going to cut off your head!"

"Then slay me too, father!" begged Manarassanah, as, weeping, she fell to her knees by Hasan's side.

To the astonishment of everyone present the old king's hand which held the sword fell to his side, and a contented smile lit his face.

When he spoke, his voice was gentle. "I was testing your love. The Almighty is compassionate and he must have ordained that your love is so strong that nothing will part you. Be happy in life and in love, my children. It is the will of Allah."

The Death of a Jester

Once long, long ago, there lived a tailor in a distant eastern town, whose trade prospered and who loved all sorts of fun and entertainment.

It so happened that one evening as he and his wife were taking a stroll near their house, they met the sultan's jester — a hunchback, renowned for his amusing jokes and unusual tricks.

The tailor greeted him and they stopped to talk. One thing led to another, and at last he invited the jester to join them at home and keep them company.

The wife honoured their guest by serving baked fish garnished with lemon and accompanied by French bread. But as the jester ate terribly slowly, concentrating all his thoughts on chewing every mouthful over and over again, and spitting out the bones, he could not at the same time entertain them with jokes and tricks. At last the wife lost her patience, seized a large slice of fish and stuffed it into the jester's mouth.

She should not have done that. A large fishbone stuck in the hunchback's throat, knocking the breath out of him, and he collapsed senseless on the floor.

No matter how hard they tried, they could not revive him. The tailor already had visions of himself swinging on the gallows, when his wife suddenly had an idea. "We'll give the hangman the slip," she said. "Don't you fret. But we must dispose of the body — it mustn't be found here. The best thing to do is to wrap it in a towel, as if it was a child and take it to that money-grabbing Jewish doctor."

The tailor gladly put his wife's bright idea into practice. They wrapped the jester in the towel, and the tailor's wife carried him like a child in her arms all the way to the doctor's. As soon as his servant opened the door, the tailor started to lament loudly, handing her at the same time a silver soin. "Hurry, hurry and call your master," he wailed between sobs. "Some terrible sickness has stricken our only son and we are helpless... oh, oh, alas!"

The slave hastened upstairs to fetch the doctor, and as soon as she was out of sight and earshot, the tailor's wife set the hunchback on the stair and hurried away, her husband running at her side.

The doctor, in the meantime, ecstatic at the sight of such a fine silver coin, ran down the stairs to see the patient. The stairway was half in darkness, so he did not see too clearly and in his haste he collided with the body of the hunchback, making him roll all the way to the front door.

"Oh, what an unfortunate man I am," he cried unhappily, when he examined the body. "Not only is it impossible for me to cure his illness, but I stand to lose my head for causing his death." And he wailed and wept over his fate, till the noise brought his wife down.

"Don't just stand here lamenting," she scolded him, "or you will truly lose your head. But why should a Jew suffer, if we can shift the blame to a Muslim? Darkness will hide us, so let us not waste time, but take that body along the roof to our neighbour!"

It so happened that the doctor's neighbour was the supervisor of the

sultan's kitchens. For some time now he had suspected that stray cats were coming in through the air shaft which led from the roof to steal his provisions.

That very evening he had armed himself with a heavy wooden club and was sitting in wait for the intruders. So when he heard suspicious rustling noises in the storeroom, followed by a loud thud, he burst inside and gave the jester one almighty blow.

A moment later he was horrified by what he had done. Instead of punishing a stray cat, he had killed a man and so put himself in the hands of the hangman!

But the kitchen supervisor also had a practical wife. "Your fate lies not in the hands of the hangman," she told him, "but in the hands of the Almighty. And he is our greatest protector. Don't waste time, but take the body out of the house at once. Only thus can you be saved!"

The supervisor therefore picked the body off the floor, tossed it across his shoulder and walked out into the street. It was almost dawn, so he had no time to wonder where he should put down his burden. He left it near the market place, resting it against a pillar, and ran off as quickly as he dared.

Even this time the poor jester was not allowed to rest in peace. A drunken Christian staggered near, and the moment he saw the body, he screamed. "Here is the thief who tried to steal my money!" With that he pounced upon the lifeless body and pummelled it with his fists in fury, till the body collapsed to the ground. He still did not stop until a guard appeared and pulled him away by force.

Then the Christian sobered up very quickly — but, alas, too late. That very morning the order went out for the gallows to be erected. After all, he had killed the sultan's jester, and now he must pay with his life.

Already the hangman's noose was round the condemned Christian's throat — his last hour had come. Suddenly a voice rose from the crowd which had gathered to watch. "Wait! The Christian is innocent! It was I who killed the hunchback!" The supervisor of the sultan's kitchens was elbowing his way through the crowd.

He stopped by the commander of the guards and said, "I already have one life on my conscience. I could not close my eyes at night, far less go on living with myself if I caused the death of another innocent man."

And he proceeded to tell his part of the story and asked for a just verdict.

"Hang him in the Christian's place!" said the commander to the hangman. But before the latter could oblige, the voice of the doctor called out from another direction, "Wait! That man is not guilty!"

What more is there to tell? Yes, the tailor too owned up that he had killed

the hunchback. The commander of the guards got more and more confused and flustered. He simply could not make up his mind which one of them to hang.

Suddenly he hit upon an idea! The dead man had been the sultan's jester, so it was up to the sultan to make the final decision, he declared. And he had all the four offenders led off to the palace.

The sultan of that land was an exceptionally strict and a just ruler. He also loved hearing unusual tales. So when the last offender had finished his confession, he pronounced, "What you all have told me is most unusual indeed, but though only one of you could have caused the death of the jester, the rest of you killed him too, if only in spirit. I shall therefore have the whole lot of you hanged — unless of course you know of someone who can think of a better, or a fairer decision."

The Christian, the Muslim and the Jew were too terrified to muster a single thought among them. But the tailor's wits had not quite forsaken him and he said, "Oh ruler of all believers, I know a certain barber who is sure to find a better solution to this problem, for he himself has experienced in life some very strange happenings."

"Fetch him then," commanded the sultan. Before long there appeared a tall, elderly man with a long flowing white beard and a thousand furrows on his brow, each furrow a sign of wisdom accumulated over many years.

"I want you to solve our problem," the sultan began, and once again the whole story was related from beginning to end, including the verdict that had been given.

"Before going further, I must see the hunchback," said the old barber after he had heard everything.

Though surprised at the request, the sultan obliged. The barber looked intently into the jester's face, and producing a pair of pincers, he forced these into the man's mouth and pulled out from far down in his throat a fishbone and a piece of meat.

As soon as this had been done, the hunchback sneezed, sat up and gazed about with bewildered eyes.

"This is the best and the most just ending to the whole story, my master," said the old barber, breaking the deadly silence.

"Truly spoken," agreed the sultan, smiling broadly. "And let this case be written down in the chronicles where it will remain forever."

The Talking Partridge

Al Malik az Zahir was one of the most noted Turkish sultans ever to rule that land. In battle he was valiant and strong, and often led his armies deep into Christian territories to spread the word and the glory of Islam. As a ruler he was fair and just.

One day he heard the rumour that his Cairo vizier had slain a wealthy, highly respected merchant for no apparent reason, and what was more, had used the man's own sword!

Al Malik shook his head in disbelief, summoned the witnesses to this dreadful deed and examined the blood-stained weapon. Everything pointed to the rumour being true. It appeared that the Cairo vizier had invited the merchant, the commander of the guards and several officers to dinner. When roast partridge was being served, the merchant was in the middle of relating an amusing story, but before he could finish, the vizier pounced upon him, tore his sword from its sheath, and in an instant the unfortunate victim was a lifeless, headless body on the floor.

The sultan could discover no further details. He therefore commanded his guards to seize the vizier and bring him before him. He ordered that the hearing would take place in the presence of several high judges.

"Only the Almighty knows all secrets," the sultan opened the court proceedings, "and we are not aware of the reason why you committed such a crime. Were you two involved in a blood feud perhaps?"

"Oh, no, ruler of all believers! That man had never sinned against me, nor harmed me in any way. I killed him on account of the story he was telling us during dinner," replied the vizier.

"Let us hear this tale, then perhaps we shall understand," said Al Malik.

"Before I begin, would you please examine the handle of the merchant's sword?" the vizier asked.

The sultan looked carefully at the expensive handle studded with pearls and gold. In the middle was a hollow space, and it was obvious that one of the jewels had fallen out of it.

"I can see something is missing," the sultan remarked. "Perhaps a pearl or a precious stone?"

"What about this diamond?" asked the vizier, opening his hand. In his palm lay a small shining stone.

The sultan took the diamond and pushed it into the empty hollow; it fitted exactly.

"Now I can proceed with the story," said the vizier, his eyes circling the courtroom. When he saw that all present were eagerly waiting, he began:

"First I must tell you that this merchant came to Cairo only a short time ago, and as all he brought with him was little in weight but high in value, he soon became one of the richest men in the city. It was the will of fate that during the dinner to which he had been invited, roast partridge was served. As soon as he saw the birds, he burst into loud laughter and said, 'I have heard it said that partridge can talk...

'Once a certain highwayman who lived by robbing caravans, was lying in wait for a lone merchant. As the rider approached, the highwayman leapt out of the bushes, pulled him off his horse and threatened him with death. The merchant begged and pleaded for his life at least to be spared. But his cries were in vain. The robber threw him to the ground, his sword raised and ready to strike. The merchant knew his last hour had come and looked around in despair. The region was bare and desolate. There was not a living thing about but a pair of partridges pecking at the grass by the wayside. "You are the sole witnesses to this bloody deed," the merchant addressed the birds. "You must denounce this murderer to those who are concerned with justice! For God cannot overlook such a crime. I offered willingly all my possessions, so that I could return to my children. But this villain will not let me live..." His words were cut short by the sharp edge of the sword...'

"I did not let my guest finish the story — for by then I knew him to be the highwayman who had murdered the merchant and robbed him of all his possessions," the vizier continued, his voice full of anger.

"I suspect that the missing diamond from the sword handle plays an important part in all this," Al Malik interrupted. "Explain it a little more clearly."

"I shall gladly oblige, for it was Allah himself who helped the truth to come out into the light of day. When that so-called merchant arrived at my house, I happened to notice there was a jewel missing from his sword handle. And at dinner, while he was telling the story, I cut into my partridge, and there inside was the missing diamond!"

"I see it all now," said the sultan. "As the highwayman struck the merchant with his sword, the force of the blow caused the diamond to fall out into the grass, and a partridge swallowed it. So Allah in his wisdom found a way for the partridge to give evidence," the sultan concluded. He remained silent, thinking of the strange paths along which justice may travel.

He released the vizier and sent him home, his honour intact. Thereupon the court hearing was closed.

The Magic Horse

In Persia there once reigned a mighty king who had three daughters and an only son. It was said that no living person could match his daughters' beauty and charm and that they were comparable only to the exquisite flowers in the royal gardens.

One day when the king was resting, three travellers came to the court and asked for an audience. Their clothes were cloaked with the same dust from their long journey, but their faces were not alike: the youngest was still in his teens, the second man in his prime, and the third — rather an ugly man — in his old age.

"We bring you precious gifts, oh King," said the middle-aged man. "They are so precious, in fact, that you won't find anything like them in the world."

"I have a golden peacock, who flaps his wings and cries at the stroke of each hour," said the young man.

"And my brass horn will sound the alarm whenever an enemy is approaching," said the man in his prime.

"My present is the most valuable of all," stated the old man. "On this horse made of ebony you can fly through the air like a bird!"

"These are truly wondrous and magnificent gifts," exclaimed the king. "How can I repay you?"

"Give us your daughters in marriage," said the three travellers, and the king agreed he would grant their request, provided that all they said of their gifts proved true.

He tested the golden peacock and it flapped its wings and with a loud cry announced the passing of that hour; the brass horn too carried out its duty and blared loudly when a band of desert thieves neared the town.

The king had two marriage contracts prepared, but he was more than a little reluctant to test the ebony horse. The ugly, bald-headed old man with the bloodshot, protruding eyes was to have his youngest and favourite daughter! He knew how grieved, how heart broken she was. He could hear the muffled sobs coming from her chamber now. But he could not bear the thought of the horse being offered perhaps to some rival ruler. Moreover, he was a king and had to keep his word.

He therefore asked for the horse to be brought to the palace courtyard and for the old man to mount him. But just then his son rushed forward crying, "Please let me try him out, Father..."

The king nodded in agreement, and the prince swung himself into the saddle, put his feet firmly in the stirrups and urged the horse forward. But the ebony animal did not move.

"Turn the knob at the right side of his neck," said the old man. He was about to give further instructions, but the impatient prince had already turned the screw. At once the horse rose from the ground and carried its rider high into the air with the speed of lightning. In a moment they became a tiny black speck to the watchers below.

The prince held on with all his strength as he saw the courtyard, the palace, the city, the fields and the desert shrink to the size of toys, then disappear altogether. He was sorry already that he had asked to test the horse himself.

Back at the palace, as soon as the king realized his son was not coming back, he stormed and raged and threatened. The old man threw himself on his mercy. "Your Majesty," he pleaded. "It is not my fault. I had no time to give the prince instructions — he flew off with such speed. It is not my fault he does not know how to direct the horse back again. But I am confident he will find the other knob which will bring the horse to the ground!"

The king was only slightly reassured, and had the old man thrown into a dark dungeon to await the prince's return.

Meanwhile the magic horse was ascending higher and higher. His flight

122

was as steady as the passage of a carrack in calm waters, and the prince relaxed a little, and began to think hard how he could get back to earth.

Turning the same knob backwards made the horse rise higher still. So he carefully examined the rest of its head and neck till he found another knob behind the horse's left ear.

He gave it a twist and the horse immediately started to lose height. Soon through the evening gloom the prince could see a foreign city below — now he could make out the streets, the squares, even the people, then they were circling above the spires of a large building.

This must be the palace, thought the prince, and gave the left knob another twist. With that the horse's downward speed increased, but nevertheless it landed gently and steadily on the firm flat roof of the palace.

123

It was dark now, and as the prince searched for a way down, he saw a light approaching, accompanied by voices and sounds of girlish laughter.

Alarmed, he drew his sword in readiness and waited. But what he saw took his breath away: a party of damsels were coming towards him, and among them a maiden of such beauty and grace that he was completely enchanted by her and could not tear his gaze away.

Her eyes too rested on the strange, handsome young man not in fear and dismay, but with interest and the first signs of love.

He stood there like a statue, hearing nothing, seeing nothing but the beautiful vision before him — till he was seized by the guards and roughly pushed along the palace passages and down its stairways. Still in a daze he found himself in a magnificent hall and realized at last he was on his knees before an angry stranger, who by his dress and manner must surely be the ruler of that land.

"Who are you that dare enter my palace unasked, that dare look upon my daughter, the princess?"

"I too have a king for a father, Your Majesty," replied the youth proudly, for now he knew certainly that he was addressing the ruler of that land.

"I do not care if you are a genie in disguise, or a true prince. Whoever you are, you will not escape punishment," stormed the king. "You have dishonoured me by coming here secretly and unannounced."

"Oh King, punish me if you will! Ask anything of me! But your palace I refuse to leave without your daughter, even if I have to fight the whole of your army to win her!"

"You've asked for it yourself," laughed the king. "Let it be so, a fight you will have. Tomorrow at dawn my soldiers will be ready!"

The prince could not sleep that night. He was not afraid of the fight to come. He knew full well the magic horse would save him whenever he so desired, but his thoughts were of the princess, of how he could win her love and carry her away.

At last the dawn was about to break and it was nearly time for battle. Row upon row of soldiers and cavalry were assembled in the meadow outside the palace, their banners flying high. To everyone's astonishment the handsome youth chose to mount his wooden horse, which had been brought down from the roof at his request.

His face suddenly lit up. For there on the balcony of her room the beautiful princess was standing gazing down with excitement and dread at all the preparations.

As the palace roof reddened with the first sunbeams, there was a roll of drums, and the ranks of cavalry, their swords glistening in the sun, started advancing towards him.

The prince waited no longer. He turned the knob to ascend and in one leap the horse was on the balcony. To the astonishment of all the spectators, he seized the princess and put her behind him, twisted the knob, and before anyone knew what was happening, they were being carried far away through the sky.

"Catch him, catch him!" cried the horrified king, when at last he found his voice. But the soldiers replied, "How can we catch a flying bird? Oh King, that young man must be a genie, or a great magician…"

At those words, and at the sight of his daughter disappearing into the clouds the agitated king collapsed senseless on the ground.

The prince, in the meantime, as he rode the ebony horse through the sky, explained to his beloved how the three strange travellers had stopped at his father's court and had given him the magic gifts; how he had asked to test the horse, which had brought him, as if drawn by destiny, to her very palace; and how it was his wish and his intention to take her home to Persia as his bride and future queen.

The princess did not protest. On the contrary, she held him all the more tightly and happily looked down at the passing rivers, fields, towns and deserts far beneath them.

The prince decided not to land in the palace courtyard, but in a far corner of the royal gardens, near a small pavilion. Once there the prince said, "It would not be fitting for the future queen of Persia to enter the palace without the welcome and the honours which are her due. Please stay here, and I shall return for you as soon as I have made all the preparations."

They bade each other goodbye and the prince left.

The old king had thought him dead, and could not believe his eyes when he appeared, alive and well. His joy and happiness were complete when he heard that his son had brought a lovely princess as his bride. The king gladly gave his consent to the marriage and all necessary arrangements were hastily made to give her the royal welcome she deserved.

In all the excitement the king did not forget the old man who had made and had given him the ebony horse. The king ordered that he be discharged from prison at once, and he promoted him to the rank of vizier. But he did not give him his daughter's hand in marriage.

The ugly old man's heart, however, was filled with hate and desire for revenge. When he overheard that the prince had not returned alone, but had brought a princess home with him on the magic horse, and that she was waiting for him in the garden pavilion, he knew this to be the perfect moment to have his revenge.

He found the ebony horse and hurried to the pavilion.

"Do not be afraid," he said with a respectful bow, when the lovely damsel eyed him with distrust and fear. "The king's son has sent me to take you to the palace on the ebony horse."

He swung himself into the saddle and lifted the unsuspecting princess in front. But all at once his bony left hand was tight over her mouth to muffle any screams, whilst the right hand was turning the knob. The horse rose like the wind and all that remained in the gardens was the echo of the old man's derisive, evil laughter.

In the palace everyone was ready to welcome the bride, and a group of female slaves walked with the prince to the pavilion, to dress her in her wedding robe.

But only silence greeted them; the garden and the pavilion were deserted. The prince searched frantically, but in vain. He dared not think what could have happened, till the king arrived and said that his newly appointed vizier was missing too. Moreover, the ebony horse was gone. It was easy then to understand what had happened. Who else would know how to handle the magic horse?

Because he was young and because he loved the princess with all his heart, the prince knew what he must do. The very next day he set out to find her, vowing that he would bring his bride back, or perish in the attempt.

He travelled and searched far and wide, going from town to town, city to city, country to country, but no one could give him news of the ebony horse, the ugly old man, or his beloved princess.

Not till he came to the distant land of the Greeks did he hear of an adventure which had befallen the very king of that country.

One day when he was out hunting, he saw a big wooden horse in a meadow. Astride it was an ugly old man who was trying to hold on to a struggling, protesting girl. When approached, the old man insisted he was her husband. But the king knew that he lied and threw him into prison, taking the enchanting damsel to live in his palace. The king would have dearly loved to marry her, but alas, she did not eat nor sleep, and seemed quite distracted. The king, grieved to see her in such a state, offered an immense reward to anyone who could cure her.

The prince thanked fate for such news and disguising himself as a physician, he knocked on the palace door. The king, who had given up all hope of the princess's recovery, received the disguised prince gladly and straight away led him to her chamber.

When he saw his beloved princess, pale, drawn and sad, his heart went out to her. Pretending to examine her, he whispered into her ear, "Please keep calm and do not show that you know me. Look at me closely. I am not a physician, but your own Prince of Persia!"

Hearing his voice and seeing through the disguise, the princess uttered a cry of joy and her eyes welled with tears of happiness.

"The patient is going to recover. As you see, she is already a little better. She needs nourishment and sound sleep. Tomorrow I shall complete the cure," the disguised prince said confidently, turning to the king.

The princess's health improved with each hour, and by that evening she was sitting up in bed, taking an interest in everything around her.

The following morning the prince said to the king of the Greeks, "To complete the cure, we must take the princess to the ebony horse which brought her here. For the horse is enchanted, and she has become bewitched by its powers. But I have no means to rid her of that spell. You must place the horse in the same meadow where you found him. You and your troops must stand some distance away. You will witness a strange spectacle, but do not fear. I swear to you that once on that horse, the princess will be completely healed in body and mind!"

The king of the Greeks was happy to oblige and soon he and his troops and crowds of people were gathered at the meadow.

The princess was carried to the horse and helped into the saddle. The prince set fire to the incense he had placed in several dishes round the horse. He then ran three times round it, reciting incomprehensible words. Soon a dark cloud of scented smoke enveloped the horse and the princess, whereupon the prince swung himself up behind her, and turned the knob...

They flew without mishap all the way back to the capital of Persia. The king, overjoyed to see them safely back, made haste with the wedding arrangements. After they were united as man and wife, they lived together for many long years in peace and in happiness.

No longer did they need the ebony horse, and the wise old king had him secretly destroyed. For though its magic had many times helped, it had also caused grief and unhappiness. It is wiser not to try changing the will of Destiny...

Abu Kir and
Abu Sir

Near the city of Alexandria lies a place called Abukir, which is a constant reminder of a certain tale about two men — Abu Kir the dyer, and Abu Sir the barber.

In those bygone, distant days they had neighbouring shops in the local square, and though they both excelled in their trade and were friends, their characters were vastly different.

Abu Sir was a serious, hard working fellow who earned respect from others, and as he was an honest, able barber, he did not lack for customers.

Now Abu Kir, the dyer, was quite a different man. He was a liar, a swindler and it was said he would rob his own grandmother of her last dinar! It was his custom, whenever someone brought material to be dyed, to demand payment in advance and then proceed to sell the stuff, usually at a profit. He would then make weak excuses and vain promises to the customers he had robbed, till eventually he closed the whole matter by swearing that some thief had stolen the material from right under his nose!

It came to pass that he became so notorious for his wicked deeds that he no longer dared to show his face in his shop. He preferred to while away the hours sitting at the barber's, safe from angry clients and their demands and protests. And what was more, at Abu Sir's he found now and then another victim simple-minded enough to fall into his snare.

But before long Abu Kir's dishonesty brought him poverty. The dye shop had to close, and he was so well known for his bad habits that nobody would let him have anything on account. As for customers, they were a thing of the past.

So he took to complaining to Abu Sir, moaning over his fate, trying at the same time to convince him how greatly to their advantage it would be if they both moved out of Alexandria, where nobody really respected their trades nor their skills. He went on and on in this vein while the barber nodded his head, but remained silent. Time went by and Abu Kir did not miss a single day in painting the rosy, prosperous future which would be theirs, if only his friend would tear himself away from his shabby existence. The barber in the end gave in to his persuasive talk and agreed to the suggestion.

They sealed their partnership by reciting verses from the Koran, vowing they would work to their mutual advantage and help each other always.

Such an agreement was greatly to Abu Kir's liking, and it did not take long for him to turn it to his own advantage.

It so happened that they boarded a ship in Alexandria which was bound for foreign lands. As they had no money for their fares or for their food, Abu Sir took out his barber's instruments and worked each day shaving the crew and cutting their hair. They repaid him with hard cash and simple food. The captain, being the richest, was the most generous, and every evening he invited both the partners to his cabin to dine at his lavish table. But Abu Kir was not really interested in such invitations. Why should he have been? After all, if he stayed on deck, he could have his fill of almost anything he fancied. He ate the simple loaves the sailors gave him as well as the selected dishes sent by the captain.

He is like a never-satisfied cannibal, Abu Sir often thought, but he let the dyer be, when Abu Kir was for ever excusing himself by saying he felt sea-sick.

After a long journey the ship moored in the harbour of a city, and the two partners found themselves lodgings ashore. The very next morning Abu Sir took all his instruments and went about the streets, practising his trade till the sun went down. He did this day after day, but the only things that Abu Kir did were sleep and rest and eat and complain that he felt giddy!

But after a few weeks the barber fell ill and was unable to go to work. Thank goodness I have a friend at hand, he thought, he is sure to look after me now. What a foolish thought!

Abu Kir certainly did not keep his part of the agreement. When he saw the money earned by the barber disappearing from the purse, he took what was left, crept out of their lodgings and left Abu Sir without any help at all.

He walked about the city, till he came to a dye shop. There was still in him a flicker of interest in his trade. He would find out how advanced they were in this city so distant from Alexandria. Also he fully realized that his bad reputation could not have followed him so far.

He was most surprised to see that all the materials had been dyed blue. It almost seemed that here in this town they did not know about all the varieties of colours, such as yellow, red, white, black, green, not to mention the different shades which Abu Kir could create on demand.

To make quite sure, he asked about it, and found his first thought was correct. This city knew no other colour but blue.

"What a chance for me," Abu Kir said to himself. "I should say it would be easy to get any dyer here to take me on, when I show what I can do." But he was wrong. He walked from one dye shop to the next till he had been to them all. As he was a foreigner, nobody wished to employ him.

Indignant and exhausted by all this exercise the dyer decided to complain to the sultan himself. And the sultan not only listened, but on hearing of Abu Kir's capabilities, he pronounced he would give the dyer a trial.

"I can see you are a master of your trade and your work will be a credit to this city. I shall tell my architects to accompany you on a tour of the town. Select the place where you want your dye shop to stand and it will be built according to your wishes."

Abu Kir was quite overwhelmed by the sultan's unexpected generosity, in fact he was quite speechless at first. But as soon as he got used to the idea, he put the sultan's plan into action. He found a convenient place, and soon a building was erected to his specifications and filled with dyes and equipment bought with the sultan's money.

Then he set to work. First he mixed many colours in different dishes, and the colours were such that their brightness and beauty almost took one's breath away. Next he took five hundred lengths of material belonging to the sultan, and dyed each one a different shade.

He worked hard and well and with pleasure. He spared no effort to complete his task. The loiterers in front of the shop were amazed at his performance, and the sultan rewarded him handsomely. From that day on orders poured into the shop, but by then he no longer worked alone. He taught the art to several slaves and he only supervised. His wealth and business grew so swiftly that soon no other dyer could compete with him. In fact many of his rivals now offered their services, but Abu Kir refused them all. He repaid their former unkindness with unkindness.

He did not give a single thought to his old friend the barber, and it did not enter his head that it was his duty, according to their agreement, to care for him during his illness.

Poor Abu Sir, in the meantime, remained weak and helpless in the little room where they had settled. When he found out that the remains of his money had disappeared with Abu Kir, he was near despair.

But what could he do? He would have surely perished if the caretaker of that lodging house had not noticed that no person had gone out or come into his room for some time. It was he who investigated and took pity on the barber, caring for him and saving him from the verge of death by giving him good food and drink.

The caretaker was the one who told Abu Sir how successful and rich his former room-mate had become, and that he was a great favourite with the sultan. And Abu Sir was overjoyed and pleased for his friend. There was no envy, no reproach in his heart and he excused the dyer's dishonesty by saying to himself that he was probably working so hard for the good of them both that he had no time to pay him a visit.

At last he recovered enough to leave his lodgings and visit the dye shop. It was easy to find — everyone seemed to have heard of it — and when he saw the building as imposing as a palace, his respect for his friend grew.

The interior matched the grand exterior. And there was Abu Kir, relaxed on cushions, clad in expensive robes, issuing orders to his workers. But the minute he saw the barber, he cried angrily, "Seize him! That is the thief, who has been stealing my materials for some time! He would have me work at a loss! Deal with him, so that he doesn't dare show his face in here again!"

Poor Abu Sir called for justice, but it was no use. He begged his friend to listen, but Abu Kir turned a deaf ear. The slaves obeyed the dyer's command and beat the barber till he was black and blue, and was hardly able to drag himself away. And while he was groaning and moaning in pain in the street, wondering how to ease his bruises, he decided that only a bath would ease the agony. But though he inquired everywhere, there was not a person in the town who had even heard of such a thing as a bath house! The only thing they could recommend was dirty sea water!

Abu Sir could scarcely believe such ignorance, which did not allow the body to be cleansed and refreshed in the proper manner. He came at last to the conclusion that the only solution was to go to the sultan and discuss the whole matter.

The sultan, who did not know the delights of a warm bath, of relaxing massage of limbs, or scented ointments, was most impressed by Abu Sir's words. He was eager that the barber should build a grand bathing place, and for this he opened wide the doors to his treasury.

The barber wasted no time. The bath house he had built was a credit to any sultan. Inside was everything anyone could want or desire — changing rooms, pools of hot and cold water with fountains rising in their centres, steam baths and private cabins. He engaged male and female slaves, picking those whose faces were beautiful and whose eyes were kind. He

taught them the art of massage, and when all was ready, he sent messengers into the town to spread the word and bring in customers. How amazed and delighted everyone was, particularly the sultan! And as Abu Sir was a just man, he demanded a fee appropriate to each individual visitor, thus making the bath house available even to the man of most meagre means. And his wealth quickly grew, and before long he was richer than Abu Kir.

The dyer soon heard of the success of his old friend. He was so consumed with envy that he pondered day and night how to harm him.

After some time he decided to visit the bath house, and after Abu Sir had welcomed him in the friendliest manner without referring to the bitter experiences of the past, the dyer said, "I have been looking for you for a long time now, for I wanted to look after you and make sure of your happiness. But now I can see that you live in luxury and don't even spare a thought for your old friend!"

It was then that Abu Sir reminded him of their last meeting, and how he had him beaten by his slaves. What a thing for a friend to do a friend! But the dyer would not own up to such a deed. How was he to recognize the haggard, skinny beggar who came to see him as his friend, the barber?

They drank coffee together and again became friends. The artful Abu Kir flattered Abu Sir with fine words, and finally said, "You have a magnificent bath house here; my dye shop cannot bring me in as much money. Just to prove to you how glad I am to see you so prosperous, I will tell you how to make your baths even more renowned. Make a mixture of lime and arsenic for your customers. It is amazing how easily it removes unwanted hair..."

"Thank you for your advice. I wouldn't have thought of such a thing. It just shows that two heads are always better than one," said Abu Sir sincerely. And so they bade each other goodbye.

The dyer, of course, was not thinking at all of helping his friend, but of harming him as much as he could. He now hastened to the sultan to warn him. "Sultan of our time! From this moment on you must not enter the bath house if you do not wish to lose your life! The barber, to whom you have given your trust and whom you have raised to the ranks of the rich, is an enemy of our faith and has prepared for you total destruction!"

"How can that be?" asked the bewildered sultan.

"If you go to the bath house, he will offer you a mixture — supposedly to remove unwanted hair. But this mixture is poisonous and would surely kill you."

The sultan did not know whether or not to believe the dyer's words, so he hurried to find out whether he had spoken the truth. And sure enough — the minute he entered the bath house, there was Abu Sir, saying, "Forgive me, Sultan, it is only now that I have remembered a certain mixture which rids the body of ugly unwanted hair, and which is in popular use in my country..."

"Show me that preparation!" the sultan commanded. When the barber brought him a rather foul smelling mixture, he began to think that this truly must be a poison prepared specially to bring about his death.

"Seize him!" he cried to the guards. And the poor unfortunate, unsuspecting man soon found himself in irons. Then he was led off to the palace, where the ruler decided that he would punish the culprit himself.

"Look at this," he said to Abu Sir, taking out of his pocket a glittering ring. "The power of this ring is such that if I put it on my index finger, and point at you, your head will fall from your shoulders. Such a death I choose for your deception and villainy."

Surprise and terror caused the blood to drain from the unhappy victim's face. But as the sultan prepared to place the ring on his index finger, it suddenly fell from his hand and rolled over to the barber's feet. Abu Sir picked it up. Everyone present looked on in horror, for now he, the condemned, was the master of life and death of all those in the palace.

Turning to the silent onlookers, he addressed the sultan, "Oh, King of the age, fate has destined me to survive your test, so I could in turn test your fairness. Therefore take back this ring."

With those words he handed the ring back to the sultan. The ruler was amazed at the barber's faith in him. Such a man surely could not be an enemy, thought he, and began to discuss the barber's crime.

Abu Sir heard the shameful tale with a sad, crest-fallen face. He then told of all his previous experiences with Abu Kir.

"How easy it is for me to see now who is the true enemy of my faith," said the indignant sultan, and added decisively, "Death, which the dyer was preparing for you, will now be his fate, as he so rightly deserves."

And that is exactly what happened. But when Abu Kir was shorter by his head, Abu Sir persuaded the sultan to allow him to take back the body of his one time friend to their homeland and have him buried there with full honour. That he did this is proved by the place near Alexandria called to this day Abukir.

The Merchant's Clever Wife and the Foolish State Officials

There are many stories about human stupidity, but in only a very few does simple common sense triumph over the powerful men of this world. This happens more easily when common sense goes hand in hand with fragile beauty...

In a certain city lived a merchant's wife as lovely as the full moon, whose glitter lights the sky. But as the merchant was so often, and for so long away on his travels, and when at home paid next to no attention to his wife, she found a lover. She managed to keep this a secret from everyone and waited only to gather together enough money for both of them to flee from the city.

It so happened that her lover struck a neighbour during a quarrel and found himself in prison.

"How could she help?" the girl wondered. Anyone who offered help would surely want something in return. Then she hit upon an idea which brought a smile to her face.

The next morning she went to see the commander of the guards and told him with tears in her eyes how the unfortunate youth, who was her own brother, came to be in jail, and how she now had not a living soul to look after her.

"That is easily rectified," replied the commander of the guards, thinking that rarely had he seen such beauty. "If you permit me to visit you this evening, your brother will be free. But first you must go and see the judge," he added.

The girl pretended to agree to all the suggestions. In fact she gave the commander such a dazzling smile that his head spun.

The judge too was smitten by her beauty, and the merchant's lovely wife promised him a meeting as well, arranging it for the same time as for the commander of the guards. The judge sent her to the vizier, to get his signature for her brother's release. The vizier too, the moment he saw her exquisite face, could think of nothing but seeing her again. So it happened that he too was given the promise of a meeting. But the vizier had not the final word in obtaining the release of the young man. That had to come from the sultan himself.

The sultan was only too pleased to sign such an order, once he was told that a visit from him would be most welcome — for even he was smitten with the girl's beauty.

"I can hardly wait for this evening to come, Sire," said the merchant's wife, bowing to the sultan.

As soon as she left the sultan's palace she turned towards the workshop of the cabinet-maker.

"I want you to make a large cupboard divided into four separate compartments," she said to him. "And one of those compartments must be enough to house... a donkey perhaps!" "I'll make it for you gladly," replied the artful cabinet-maker, "but may I call personally at your house tonight to collect payment?"

"By all means come," the girl agreed. "But in that case make five

separate compartements in the cupboard, and deliver it this afternoon."

The cabinet-maker was only too pleased to say yes — why not, when a customer was as beautiful as this girl? He set to work with enthusiasm.

The merchant's wife also did not waste time. She went to the market to buy drinks and food for her distinguished guests. She then rummaged among discarded clothes till she found four old robes which she took to the dyer, instructing him to dye each one a different colour.

Before she knew it, daylight was gone. She just managed to put the new cupboard in the right place, sprinkle herself with perfume and comb her hair — and there was the commander of the guards knocking on her door, dressed in his best clothes.

The girl showed her respect by kissing the ground at his feet, then led him to the table laden with delicious food and drinks. When after dinner

141

they washed their hands and the commander wished to embrace her, she said, "First I want you to feel comfortable, so please put on this robe." And she handed him one of the dyed garments. The impatient commander was changing hurriedly, when there was another knock on the door.

"Who can that be?" he asked.

"My husband must have returned!" she cried in terror. "He must not find you here, or he would kill you for sure... You must hide in the cupboard! Hurry!"

So the commander found himself in the bottom compartment of the new cupboard. It was the judge who was now standing at the door. And soon he was followed by the vizier and the sultan. The girl managed to get them all to change into the dyed old robes and lock them in different compartments.

The cabinet-maker was the last to arrive. As soon as he was inside, she attacked him, "So you've come to collect your pay? I don't think you have earned it, for I can't get anything into that fifth compartment!"

"It is so big that I would fit into it," objected the cabinet-maker.

"Prove it to me then!" said the girl, opening the fifth door. The minute the craftsman was in, she turned the key in the lock.

What happened next?

Naturally enough, the merchant's wife wasted no time. As soon as dawn broke, she went to the market and sold the beautiful clothes of the commander, the judge, the vizier and the sultan. Armed with all the signatures, she soon had her sweetheart released, and the two of them ran away and were never seen or heard of again.

But all those state officials locked in the cupboard were not so happy. Afraid of the disgrace and ridicule, they did not dare utter a sound.

Eventually, fear that they might perish without air and in darkness in their cramped compartments made them discuss the matter and decide to call for help.

At first those who came to see what all the noise was about were afraid to open the cupboard. After all, evil spirits could have been locked in it — but in the end, when the judge recited lines from the Koran, which is something that no evil spirit would do, they let the prisoners out.

What a sight they were! Dressed in the bright, tattered robes the artful girl had got ready for them, they looked so silly and ridiculous, that they became the laughing stock of the whole town. And although they carried on ruling the people in their official capacity, they had lost everyone's respect.

The Evil Brothers

It so happened that during the reign of Haroun al Raschid, Abdallah Fadil, the emir of Basra, had not sent in his taxes which were due.

Haroun thought there must be a good reason for the emir's lapse, for Abdallah was one of his most honoured, reliable subjects. He decided therefore to go to Basra to see for himself.

Abdallah received him with many apologies, assuring him the payment to the caliph was ready. And as the presence of such an honourable guest demands, he organized a huge feast for Haroun and his retinue which continued into the night.

When it was time to retire, the emir ordered that a bed be prepared by his own so that they might rest side by side.

Haroun could not sleep, but pretended he was no longer awake. So it was that he heard Abdallah rise and leave the bedroom. He too left his bed and, unseen, followed at a distance, curious to see what his friend would do. They went through several long passages till the emir came to a spacious hall, thickly carpeted, in the centre of which was a large divan framed in ebony. To the caliph's surprise two black hounds were tied to the frame with gold chains.

As soon as they saw Abdallah, they barked and wagged their tails, showing how pleased they were to see him. But the emir picked up a whip and beat them both with such force, that they fell into unconsciousness. Yet afterwards he stroked them gently, soothing them with his own hand, and gave them drink and food, whilst all the time he said prayers for them. At last he took the candle and returned to his chamber.

Though such behaviour seemed most strange to Haroun, all the next day he gave no sign, nor mentioned what he had witnessed.

But when the episode was repeated the following night and on the third night too, the caliph could no longer hold back his curiosity. On the third morning, when they had breakfasted and prayed, he said, "Emir Abdallah, I have been destined to find out about your two black hounds and about the strange way you treat them. You must tell me truthfully what it all means. Why do you beat them into unconsciousness and why afterwards do you treat them as if they were of your own blood?"

"They truly are of the human race, apostle of God," Abdallah replied respectfully. "But so that you may know the entire truth, I shall have to relate the whole story, and have the dogs for witnesses."

Haroun al Raschid was only too pleased to agree to such a suggestion. So the emir fetched both the hounds and began his tale:

"I am the youngest of three sons of a wealthy merchant Fadil. My father called his first-born Mansur, and my second brother is named Nasir.

"We had a very happy childhood, but as soon as we grew up, our father fell ill and then passed away. He left us much wealth in the form of money and possessions, also a spacious house and a prosperous business.

"It was after the funeral, when all the slaves had been released, the Koran had been read and the alms had been distributed to the poor, that I asked my brothers whether they wished all the possessions to be split into

145

three parts, or whether they wanted to remain under the same roof and live together as before.

"Mansur and Nasir both asked for their shares. So they were given the money and goods. To me they left the house and the business of their own free will, and went off to seek their fortunes in a distant land.

"It was in winter, exactly a year later, when I was busily working, that they suddenly returned. Without a single dinar, starving and trembling with cold, I gave them my fur coats and fed them well. And they told me how they went into business in Cairo and Baghdad, making great profits, and how when they were aboard a ship sailing back to Basra, they were caught in a violent storm and were lucky to escape with their lives. It was in poverty therefore that they made the rest of their way home, begging for food to keep alive. At last they reached their old home.

"I listened to all their complaints against a merciless fate and said to them, 'Dear brothers, whilst it was your destiny to suffer on your travels, God showed his generosity to me. He allowed me to enlarge my property by business dealings to the same size as it was at the time of our father's death and before we split it into three parts. Take a third each once again. I am confident you will do better.'

"I acted on my decision. Mansur and Nasir worked as merchants again, but this time I insisted that they remained in Basra, so that I could keep my eye on them. But although their earlier journey had been full of bitter experiences, they were not content, but thirsted for adventures and easy riches in distant lands.

"They managed to convince me, so that I gave in to their wishes and after thorough preparations all three of us set off on our voyage.

"We hired a ship and loaded it in Basra with merchandise to be sold in other places, and in this ship we sailed along the coast from town to town.

"But though we made easy profit by buying and selling, we met not only good fortune, but also misfortune.

"One day we ran out of water on board. We anchored off a small island and went in search of a spring. I climbed a hill, and there witnessed a very unequal struggle. A black dragon was pursuing a helpless white snake. It caught up with the snake and buried its talons in the snake's body. Unable to bear such an unfair fight, I seized a large stone and struck the dragon with such force it fell down dead on the spot.

"To my amazement the white snake in that instant turned into a beautiful damsel who walked over to me and said, 'It is thanks to you,

Abdallah, that I am saved. I am the genie Saida. If ever you are in trouble, you too will have help from me...'

"Thereupon the earth parted and she disappeared.

"My brothers, in the meantime, had found water, so we set sail again. Some days later the captain brought the ship to another foreign shore, so that we might replenish our supplies.

"Not far from the place where we anchored I saw large imposing city with high walls, fortifications and iron gates. Surely here we could get everything we needed!

"But when I inquired who would accompany me to the city, they all refused, even my own brothers. Such a plan was most dangerous, they said, for only unbelievers lived in these regions, and to put ourselves in their hands could only lead to disaster.

"What else could I do but go on my own? I relied on destiny and put myself in the hands of the Almighty. I set out towards the city gates, not knowing what to expect. Reality surpassed all expectations. Every single person I came across, from the guard by the gates to the merchants, tradesmen, soldiers, ordinary men and women in the market, as well as the viziers, the sultan and the sultana in the palace — everyone in that city had been turned to stone! I could gather as much gold, silver and precious stones as I desired. But as soon as I touched anything, it turned to dust — so rotten was it with the passing of time.

"I wandered about the palace chambers, finding only deathly stillness and everywhere signs of the abrupt, unexpected end of activities. Suddenly my ears caught the melodious whisper of a girlish voice, reciting verses from the Koran, the only human voice left in the whole city!

"Curious to see the owner of the voice speaking words which sounded to me like heavenly music, I went on and came face to face with a maiden more beautiful than a fresh rosebud, her radiance equal to that of the sun.

"The maiden, who was reclining on soft cushions, rose and greeted me like an old friend, 'Peace be with you, Abdallah, the delight of my eye!'

"It was with difficulty that I hid the excitement I felt at seeing such beauty. But I could not hide my curiosity and I showered her with questions, wanting to know how she came to know me and my name, and why it was that she was the only human being alive in this city turned to stone.

"In reply she told me a story which explained everything that I had so far seen:

148

"Her father, apparently, was a mighty ruler of a large kingdom and during his reign he amassed a huge fortune. But instead of thanking the one and only God for his good fortune, he worshipped an idol made by human hand from precious stones. And all the dignitaries, the wealthy citizens, the soldiers, the simple folk, in short all the inhabitants of the whole kingdom worshipped similar images.

"It so happened that one day a traveller dressed in green entered the palace, his face lit by the holy radiance of believers. It was he who reprimanded the king for worshipping idols and urged him to become a Muslim. Not only did the king not heed the stranger's words, but tried to bring about his destruction. The king ordered that all idols be brought into the palace and placed side by side, till there was no space left.

149

"Then the king and all his subjects fell to their knees before their gods, praying that their wrath would pursue the stranger.

"But the traveller's faith proved too strong for them. No harm came to him, but he in turn knocked down the king's idol, and with outstretched hands asked his own God to turn the unbelievers to stone. And in that instant the whole city was turned to stone — except for the king's daughter. She escaped this terrible fate because she was predestined by Allah to turn to the true faith.

"The Muslim stranger then introduced the princess to the teachings of the Koran and it was he who also foretold that I would venture into her city, and would lead her away as my wife.

"I returned to my ship with many precious things. Radji my wife was the greatest treasure of all.

"Even my brothers could not take their eyes off her, and demanded that I gave her to them. Then I realized for the first time how greedy and selfish they were. I divided the jewels and gold fairly among us, but refused to share Radji. I guarded her closely till the spires of Basra appeared on the horizon.

"I was sure that then all would be well, that no disaster could occur, and I gave way to drowsiness. I slept.

"This was what Mansur and Nasir were waiting for. They seized me and tossed me overboard into the foaming waves. I was bidding this world goodbye, when suddenly I was helped by someone I had almost forgotten. It was the genie Saida. She had been constantly watching over me, hoping to repay the debt she felt she owed me after I saved her from the dragon.

"Turning into a huge bird, she plucked me from the vicious waves and in a trice put me down on the deck of the ship.

"Alas, it was too late, for when Radji realized what had happened, she plunged into the sea after me. Only my own brothers were standing there, gaping in terror and astonishment to see me alive. But they soon regained their composure and embraced me heartily, as if they had not tried to end my life.

"Saida then stepped in. She wanted to punish them with death there and then for their wicked deed. It took all my efforts to persuade her to spare at least the life of my brothers.

"So she turned them into these low hounds and instructed me to beat them each night into unconsciousness, warning me that if I disobeyed, I would be whipped by her.

"This was what happened the very first night, when I did not heed the order. Even today, after twelve years, I can still feel the blows of her whip, so I no longer forget her instructions.

"So thus is my story, oh Caliph," Abdallah ended with a sigh, and bowed his head.

"What an unusual tale," remarked Haroun al Raschid, and asked, "Have you forgiven your brothers?"

"Why, of course, my master! All I ask now is that they forgive me for all the beatings I have had to give them. Everything else depends on God."

"In that case I shall instruct Saida to take away her curse," the caliph announced. He wrote a letter, sealed it and handed it over to Abdallah, saying, "Free your brothers from their chains and do not beat them again. When Saida comes, you must not be afraid, but give her this letter..."

Abdallah then bade Haroun goodbye, showering him with thanks. When the caliph and his attendants had disappeared from sight, he turned back. He unchained the dogs straight away, and ordered a lavish table to be prepared for him and for them.

The servants and guards thought their master must have gone out of his mind, to dine with beasts, and they refused to touch the remains from the feast. But Abdallah paid no attention to their objections, and had beds prepared for his dog-brothers alongside his own.

Suddenly the ground opened and Saida stood there.

"Why have you freed the hounds? Why are you honouring such traitors, instead of beating them? Would you like me to turn you into a dog too?" she cried, her eyes gleaming with anger.

The emir handed over the letter from Haroun al Raschid and she read it carefully.

"I am the daughter of the king of the genies," Saida then said, "and I cannot act without my father's permission. Wait till I have consulted him. I shall let you know his decision presently..."

Saida then disappeared, but soon she was back.

"You shall have your way," she said, "for the caliph of the believers has also great powers over us. But I warn you, your brothers are false and treacherous and will bring you no good."

With that she poured some liquid into a bowl, muttered a few words of a magic formula and sprinkled the liquid on both the dogs.

Immediately Mansur and Nasir stood before them, youthful and handsome as of old. There was much joy and rejoicing, laughter and happy tears and none of them noticed that Saida disappeared. They drank together and talked and celebrated till the break of dawn, when they all set out to see the caliph.

Haroun al Raschid received both the culprits graciously and showered gifts upon them, though at the same time he reprimanded them for their past wickedness.

So it came about that after twelve years Mansur and Nasir began living again the life of human beings. Abdallah made them his assistants, bought them magnificent houses and found them beautiful wives. His kind heart forgot all past sorrows and grievances.

The brothers, however, though they behaved warmly and lovingly towards Abdallah, nursed only hate and envy in their hearts. They had not learned their lesson. They were jealous that their brother was an emir, highly

honoured by the people. They were furious that no one showed them such respect and thought that if they could only get rid of their brother, the caliph might make them the joint emirs of Basra.

Their hate grew day by day, till they could bear it no longer, and they agreed to kill their brother. They invited him to Mansur's house, which stood by the river. There they prepared many highly intoxicating drinks for the occasion.

The unsuspecting Abdallah came gladly, and soon was talking with them merrily, raising the glass to his lips constantly. His brothers made sure it was always full.

It was very late when Abdallah fell into a deep sleep in his chair. But Mansur and Nasir were wide awake. They were on their feet like lightning as soon as they heard their brother's loud, regular breathing. Now was the moment to pounce on their helpless victim and strangle him.

At last they thought they had achieved their evil intention, as they dragged the lifeless body onto the terrace and threw it into the river.

The next morning both these evil plotters went to see the caliph Haroun al Raschid. Falling on their knees, their eyes full of tears, they explained that Abdallah's deeds had angered the genie Saida and that she had carried him away from this world.

But they underestimated the caliph's wisdom and character. The ruler immediately summoned the genie to justify her action.

And the daughter of the king of the genies said, "Oh King of all believers, how true my words of warning were regarding these treacherous brothers.

Why, they themselves strangled Abdallah and threw him into the river, so that the water would close over him forever and hide their guilt. Happily they did not complete their evil deed. Abdallah was not dead, but unconscious. So before he sank to the river bed, I changed into a large fish and carried him to the opposite shore, where he is now recovering."

Hearing this, the caliph became so angry that he gave an immediate order for justice to be carried out. Mansur and Nasir that very day were beheaded before Abdallah's palace.

What in the meantime was happening to their brother? On the far shore of the river, consciousness did not return to him until it was bright daylight. There was not a living soul about — all he could see was an endless, sandy plain.

An hour or so later his eyes were gladdened by the sight of an approaching caravan. They would surely have pity and help him.

And they did. He was made comfortable, fed and clad. And the leader of the caravan, who had studied how to heal the sick, attended to Abdallah himself.

So it happened that after one month of travelling Abdallah came into the land of Persia. He had still not completely recovered, so they spent that night in a lodging house. There the emir was told of a pious, learned woman who lived in a nearby hermitage, who knew how to cure all illnesses and who was therefore visited by the sick from near and far.

Sick as he was, Abdallah set out to see her. From inside, as he approached he heard a voice, a well-known, long unheard, beloved voice.

"Welcome to you, Abdallah!" it said.

Yes! It was Radji, the light of his world, the beloved of his heart, whom he had once led him from the city of stone.

They had so much to tell one another! Abdallah learned that the traveller in green, who had turned her father to stone, had rescued her from the sea and had taught her how to cure all illnesses — and he also had foretold the day of their reunion.

What more is there to tell?

Abdallah immediately recovered completely, and with the help of the pious traveller they both returned to Basra. There they learned of the just punishment which had met the evil brothers. The caliph, overjoyed at seeing them, had the marriage agreement speedily prepared, and from that day on they were never again parted.

The Tomcat and the Mouse

The weather was wet and miserable, but Tom the tomcat was so hungry he had to forsake his nice warm den and brave the elements in search of food.

The rain poured down in torrents; there wasn't a bird to be heard and all mice seemed to have disappeared from the face of the earth. There wasn't even a single fly to be seen — and the poor bedraggled tomcat ran hither and thither all for nothing. He grew so weak that his little legs grew more and more unsteady while his furry coat was like a sea-soaked sponge.

He was nearly at the end of his tether and thought his last hour had surely come, when he noticed a mousehole in the roots of a mighty oak. He peeped inside without much hope, but next moment his spirits rose. For there, before his very eyes, was a real mouse, a fat little mouse. Her back was turned towards him and she was digging up the soil with her little front paws for all she was worth, doing her best to block the entrance against unwelcome visitors.

"I have no wish to harm you," miaowed the tomcat in what was left of his voice. "I just want to come in and get warm."

The mouse stopped piling up the soil, but replied, her eyes suspicious, "How could I and my worst enemy be together? It's like adding wood to the fire, or asking a thief to look after my money. No! Certainly not! You can't come in! We've been deadly enemies since time began!"

"If you forgive me, I am sure we can be friends and I shall never harm you again!" promised Tom the tomcat, his voice gentle and sweet as honey. "Surely you must know that if you show kindness to any of God's creatures, our Creator will show kindness to you!"

"Why should I throw myself on your mercy?" asked the mouse. "You are, after all, a hundred times stronger than I, and your sharp teeth could snap me in two whenever such a thought came into your head."

"How can I convince you, little mouse, that I am utterly miserable and feel near to death... I cannot force myself to walk another step, and this terrible rain will kill me in no time at all. I am done for, I tell you, unless you let me come in. And if I drop dead, in the eyes of the Maker you'll be to blame!" wailed the tomcat with such a heartbreaking miaow that the mouse was now really frightened.

For whoever wishes to have the Almighty on his side must show generosity and give help even to an enemy in need. Otherwise he or she is faced with destruction...

So she widened the opening and helped Tom inside.

The tomcat could barely breathe, so weak was he, and the mouse cared for him to the best of her ability. But after a time, when he felt the old strength returning to his muscles and bones, the artful tomcat barred her way to the outside world. Pulling her to him roughly with his claws, he said, leering into her frightened face, "You are a crazy fool to help an enemy. You don't deserve a better fate than death!"

With that he proceeded to taunt her and play with her in the true cat and mouse fashion — tossing her up in the air, letting her run a few steps, then pouncing on her, till the poor little thing squeaked piteously with terror.

Her cries were heard by a hunting dog, who was sniffing around nearby. A fox, thought he, licking his lips, and he bounded to the mousehole and pulled out the ungrateful tomcat, the mouse gripped in his mouth.

Tom the tomcat was now filled with an awful dread and he dropped the mouse — who was, thank Heavens, still alive. But that did not save the tomcat's life. The hunting dog with one bite killed him.

This story shows that help comes to those who show kindness and mercy. But the ones who have only violence in mind are usually justly repaid in kind.

Ali Baba and
the Forty Thieves

In a certain town of Persia there once lived two brothers, one called Cassim, the other Ali Baba. Their father had died leaving them little inheritance, and by the time they divided it between them, neither could be said to be anything but poor. Fate, however, had different futures for them both. The elder brother, Cassim, married the daughter of a rich merchant and turned very greedy and envious, whereas Ali Baba took for a wife a woman as poor as a church mouse. He was honest and hard working, but never succeeded in making money. Soon he did not know where their next meal was coming from. All he had left was the roof over their heads, a good and handsome son, a willing donkey and determination not to give up.

The only way he could still make a dinar or two was by felling wood in the forest and selling it in town. He toiled from morning till night, his patient donkey at his side waiting to bring the logs back into the town. And in this way one day wearily followed another, and he was just able to scrape together enough to keep hunger away from the door of their miserable house.

One day when he was working in the forest, he saw a cloud of dust in the distance, followed by the sound of galloping hooves. He watched, his eyes following the cloud, till it came closer and he saw it was a band of wild looking riders, gleaming swords and daggers in their belts. The sight made Ali Baba hold his breath in terror. There must have been at least forty of them in all.

Ali Baba, his heart in his mouth, left the donkey to its fate and dived into the bushes, and when he was sure nobody was watching, he climbed into the crown of a tall oak tree. From there he could see everything unobserved.

The riders dismounted at the foot of the tree which grew by a large rock. Ali Baba guessed by the look of them that these men must be thieves — and dangerous ones at that. Each of the riders took off their saddle bags and turned to the rock which was overgrown by thistles and weeds.

And there the tallest of them — by his bearing and attire the leader — cried, "Open, Sesame!"

To Ali Baba's astonishment the rocky wall shook and rattled and a door opened. The robbers entered, one by one, their leader last of all. Then the door closed behind them.

Ali Baba waited without daring to move for some time, before the mysterious riders reappeared. Ali Baba could not help noticing that their saddle bags were now slack and empty, and he had a better opportunity to examine their faces. They were unshaven, scarred and furrowed with cruel lines and creased brows which made him shudder. This surely must be the notorious evil band of robbers who had terrorized the whole region for so long!

They all walked over to their horses, hung their bags over their saddles, and remounted. Soon they disappeared in a cloud of dust. Ali Baba followed them with his eyes, not daring to descend till they were well out of sight.

When all was quiet and still, he climbed down and sighed with relief.

Now he was curious to see what was inside the cave. It seemed to him that the robbers must be using it as a hiding place for their booty.

"Open, Sesame," he called, for he remembered the words of command the leader had uttered. The door opened, and he entered.

The rock closed fast behind him, but this did not worry Ali Baba, for after all, he knew well how to get out again.

To his surprise he did not find himself in a dark, eerie place. He was in a bright, spacious vault, filled with piles of gold, jewels, rich stuffs from India and China, carpets and a heap of leather purses filled with money. "If I toiled with a spade for a whole day, I couldn't move all that," thought the dazed Ali Baba. He walked from wall to wall of that great cave, his head spinning, his eyes dimmed by the dazzling glitter. The enormous quantities of riches convinced Ali Baba that this cave had been used as a thieves' hiding place for many years.

But he did not dare waste time on dreams and thoughts. He had to get out, for he was much afraid that the robbers might return. Ignoring all else, he walked over to the bags of gold and gathered up as many as he could carry. Then he commanded the rock, "Open, Sesame!"

Once outside he loaded the bags on the donkey's back, placing some logs on top to hide them from view, and set off for home.

The moment he arrived home, he locked the door behind him, to make sure no uninvited guest would enter and catch him unawares. Then, to his wife's astonishment, he emptied all the bags of gold one by one onto the floor. The bewildered woman was too stunned to utter a single word, but eyed him suspiciously, wondering if her husband had turned thief. Ali Baba soothed her, explaining where it had come from and told her that the gold was only a small portion of the treasure which had been stolen by a band of wicked robbers. Once reassured, she recovered and stifling her fears, was most anxious to count the gold.

"That would be an impossible task," her husband objected. "You would not be finished by the morning. It is not safe to have this money lying about so long. I must hide it straight away. The best idea is to dig a hole in the garden and bury it." The wife agreed, but still insisted she must first find out how rich they now were. So she persuaded her husband to wait a little, then ran over to Cassim's house, which was nearby, to borrow his grain measure. Cassim was out, but his wife was glad to oblige.

"Certainly you may borrow the measure," she said. "Wait here, I will fetch it."

But all that time she was wondering what grain Ali Baba needed to weigh, when he was so poor. Curiosity made her stick some wax at the bottom of the measure, then she handed it over, apologizing for taking so long.

Whilst Ali Baba was busily digging the hole in the garden, his wife filled the measure with gold ten times over. Then happy and satisfied, she looked on as her husband poured it into the hole he had dug and covered it up with a thick layer of soil.

That same evening Cassim's wife had the measure back in her possession. As soon as she was alone, she looked inside, and to her amazement found a shining gold coin sticking to the bottom.

"Oh that artful Ali Baba!" she cried, and ran to Cassim to tell him of her discovery. "Your brother is living and behaving as if he was a pauper," she gasped, "and all the time he's far wealthier than you! He has so much gold, in fact, that he doesn't count it, but weighs it!"

Cassim was a true miser who hated parting with a single dinar, and who envied anyone who had anything that could be envied. Greediness did not let him have a wink of sleep that night. And all the time his head was buzzing with one question. How had Ali Baba acquired all that money?

The next day, he quickly mumbled his morning prayer and then rushed off to his brother's house. He hammered on his door. Ali Baba greeted his older brother most cordially. But Cassim immediately flew into a rage. Loudly he abused him, calling him a two-faced brother, a liar and a cheat, accusing him of pretending to be poor. "Look at you", he shouted at last. "Anyone would think you were a miserable pauper without a possession in the world. But I know the truth! You have to weigh your gold with the grain measure, because you have too many gold coins to count. See here," he added, producing the tell-tale coin. "Here is my proof. My wife found this piece of gold in the measure you borrowed. Now either you admit it and tell me everything, or I swear I'll march you off to the judge immediately and accuse you of being a thief."

"I shall be only too pleased to explain everything," said Ali Baba smoothly, swallowing his anger. He realized his secret was discovered and that he had no choice but to relate to his brother the events of the previous day. He even offered to share with Cassim the gold he had taken, as long as he kept the secret. And he described the very spot where the rock Sesame could be found.

"I do not advise you to go there, dear brother. That would be tempting

162

Providence," he warned him. "It is better for us to be content with what I have brought than to risk falling into the hands of those terrible bandits."

But the greedy, conceited Cassim only smiled haughtily. "Why should I be such a fool as to be satisfied with so little, when there is a hundred times more wealth to be had? I'm not one to let such an opportunity slip through my fingers!"

Ali Baba reluctantly gave in and told his brother the magic formula. That was all Cassim needed. Hurriedly he left his brother's house and spent the rest of the day buying up all the mules in the town, till the townsfolk began to wonder if he planned to deprive the mule-sellers of their livelihood.

Once again Cassim could hardly wait for morning to come, and before daybreak he was already climbing with his caravan of mules up the hills

and through the forest towards the rock which Ali Baba has described.

"Open, Sesame!" he called, as he came to the secret door. And the rock wall opened. Cassim went inside and behind him the door closed.

Everything he saw was just as Ali Baba had described. There were riches here to fill all the boxes and bags he had brought, and there would be still more to return for! Dazed and excited he ran about the cave, examining the gold, the jewels, fingering the exquisite cloths, feasting his eyes on all the wealth that now was his. Then he started to carry the sacks of gold and precious stones and bales of materials to the entrance where he could load them on to the donkeys more easily. So consumed with greed was he that he thought of nothing else but riches.

When at last he remembered that he should be returning home, he found to his dismay that he had forgotten the name of the rock! He knew it was some kind of a grain — but which one? He called out "Open, Barley!" then "Open, Corn!", even "Open, Oat!" and hopefully "Open, Wheat!" till he had named every type of grain, except one — sesame.

And so the rock remained firmly closed, and the greedy Cassim, now almost out of his mind with terror, started shouting for help. Too late he realized that he should have listened to his younger brother's warning.

To add to his horror he heard the tramping of hooves — the thieves had returned! They could not fail to notice the mules waiting patiently by the cave's entrance. They would know at once that some intruder was inside.

"Open, Sesame!" the bandit captain commanded angrily, his sword ready in his hand. As the door began to open, the desperate Cassim tried to dive past. But before he could even glimpse the light of day, the thieves slew him, showing no mercy. They dragged his body back inside the cave, where they cut it into quarters and hung these up on each side of the entrance — to deter anyone else who might wish to enter.

Then the robbers drove the mules off into the forest, and put back in place all the treasures Cassim had stacked by the door. Last they added the load they had robbed from a caravan that day.

Soon only a cloud of dust told of the whereabouts of the thieves, and as they galloped away the dust too disappeared, and the whole region was as quiet and still and empty as before.

When Cassim failed to return home, his wife became anxious. When she could not bear the worry any longer she ran to Ali Baba's house and told him that Cassim had not come home. Ali Baba was almost sure his brother had gone to the cave, and now was very much afraid that the robbers might

164

have found him in or near their cave. He did not wait to be asked to search for Cassim, but as soon as he had soothed his sister-in-law, he took three donkeys and set out for the forest.

He made straight for the fateful rock. Cautiously he looked around, and trying to avoid stepping on any twigs, he crept noiselessly closer. Soon he was satisfied there was no one about.

"Open, Sesame!" he spoke the magic words.

Oh, horror of horrors! What a sight met his eyes! There to right and to left hung his brother's remains. Now he knew with dreadful certainty that mercy would be shown to no man who crossed the path of these evil thieves.

In spite of the fact that Cassim had never been a good brother to him, and that there was danger that he too might be trapped by the thieves, Ali Baba was determined to bury him as a believer with full honours and respect. So he wrapped the remains in a rich cloth and loaded them on one of his asses. He covered the bundle with brushwood to hide it from curious eyes. The other two donkeys he loaded with bags of gold, and these too he covered with brushwood. Then he ordered the door to close behind him and set off quickly for home.

It was nightfall by the time he drove the donkeys up to his house. He told his wife to unload the gold and to bury it, while he led the third donkey bearing Cassim's corpse to his sister-in-law's house.

Thoughts raced through Ali Baba's head — thoughts which chilled and horrified him. What was going to happen when the robbers discovered that the corpse had gone? They would surely find his tracks and trace him to his home.

He was still shaking with terror as he knocked on the door of Cassim's house. It was opened by Morgiana, his brother's highly trustworthy maid.

Swearing her to secrecy, Ali Baba told her the whole story. When he had finished, Morgiana remained silent for a time, deep in thought. At last her face lit up, and she said, "I know what we must do! We shall pretend that my late master is not dead, but critically ill. I will hurry to the chemist in great distress and ask for medicine. And tomorrow we shall pretend that poor Cassim has died a natural death during the night, and we will bury him with full honours."

"I knew I could rely on you," Ali Baba whispered with a sigh of relief. "But what about the body? It is in pieces..."

"That is of no consequence," Morgiana assured him. "I will bribe a cobbler to sew the pieces together again, and no one will be any the wiser.

You'd be surprised what a gold coin in the hand will do! And to make quite sure he'll keep his mouth closed, I will blindfold him when I bring him here. And while I am attending to all this, you had better inform Cassim's wife of her loss, and ask her to marry you. You are allowed, after all, more than one wife, and in that way you can remain one family."

Ali Baba at once carried out Morgiana's instructions. Cassim's wife, grief-stricken at first, did not wish to remain a widow for long and was only too glad to accept Ali Baba's proposal. Her late husband's body was duly sewn together by a rather frightened cobbler. His fears were, however, somewhat calmed by the feel of the gold coin in his pocket. Cassim was then placed in a coffin and buried with the usual rituals. After the funeral, Ali Baba moved to his new wife's house, took over the running of Cassim's business and settled happily into the role of a prosperous citizen.

But in the meantime the thieves were not wasting time.

When they discovered that Cassim's corpse was missing, together with several sacks of gold, they were convinced that the dead man must have had an accomplice who knew their hideout and the secret formula.

"We must track down this other man and kill him at once. Otherwise neither we, nor our treasure will ever be safe," said the captain. "I want the boldest and the cleverest man to disguise himself as a merchant, ride into the city and find out if anyone has died suddenly and recently."

The chosen man did not take long to discover that the citizen Cassim had been struck by a sudden illness and had recently died, and that Ali Baba, his brother, had turned from a pauper into a very prosperous man.

The clever robber did not have to be told more.

Soon he was standing in the street, facing the late Cassim's house. All the buildings in that street looked exactly alike. "I could easily make a mistake in the dark," the thief thought to himself. So he marked the front door with a cross in white chalk. Then he hurriedly returned to the forest in the hills, where he told the captain how cleverly he had arranged everything.

But he did not take into account the intelligent Morgiana.

Soon after the thief had gone, Morgiana went out to the market. She noticed immediately the chalk mark on the door, and though she thought it might be the work of some mischievous children, she did not rule out the possibility that an enemy of her new master could be responsible. So to make quite sure she took a piece of chalk and marked all the doors in the street with similar crosses.

In the forest in the meantime the robbers were making their plans. The

captain was very pleased with his scout's discovery. He was now determined to lead the whole band of robbers to Ali Baba's house. And so, disguising themselves in the cloaks of respectable merchants, they waited for night to fall. In darkness they set out, their sharpened swords hidden by the folds of their cloaks. They little guessed what a surprise was waiting for them. When they discovered that all the doors in the street where Ali Baba lived were marked exactly alike, the captain grew angry, and ordered his men to retreat back to the woods.

Once by the rock they held a meeting to decide how to punish the clumsy scout whose plan had so miserably failed. "We shall judge him according to our custom," the captain spoke, and the others nodded their heads in agreement. The condemned man knew he could not live with his shame, and that his hour had come. He bent his head fearlessly and willingly, and it was chopped off there and then. For among thieves there is an understanding that whoever fails in his duty must perish.

Another volunteer rose now. This was Ahmad, the strongest and the most daring of them all. "Fellow comrades," he said, "for such a task I am the most suitable; if I fail to lead you to the right place, let me face the same fate as that of my former comrade."

"So be it, Ahmad," said the captain. "If you fulfill your promise, all the spoils in Ali Baba's house shall be yours. If you do not, then we shall have your head."

But Ahmad fared no better. He did find the right house, and instead of marking it with white chalk, he stained it in a most inconspicuous place with a drop of his own blood. But the observant Morgiana noticed the little red mark, when she returned home from the market carrying fresh fish. She lost no time, but marked all the doors in the street with the same little red spot, using the blood of the fish she had bought for her purpose. Now she was quite certain that her suspicions were correct, and that someone was trying to kill her master.

When the gang of the thieves had gone back to town and had realized they had been fooled once again, the captain was filled with terrible fury. Ahmad was soon shorter by his head and the captain was at a loss what to do next. "My men are excellent robbers, but have few brains," he thought. "If I continue like this I'll lose them all."

So he decided on different tactics.

"I myself shall tackle the problem tomorrow morning," he roared at his men. "And I shall not allow myself to be fooled. While I am gone, you will

buy twenty mules, and forty large oil containers. But make sure you fill only two of them with oil. The others you must leave empty," he added threateningly.

The captain then dismissed his men and the thieves, glad to escape from their chief's rage, crept away like dogs after a beating. There was little sleep for them that night, as they waited uneasily for morning to break.

The captain soon found out which house in the street belonged to Ali Baba. He did not mark it with any sign, but gazed at it for a long time, memorizing every detail. Then to make doubly sure, he counted the houses first from one end of the street, then from the other, till he came to the home of the man he wanted. Now he knew he could not make a mistake. Before dusk gathered, he was back in the hills with his men.

The robbers had been busy and everything was ready. There were nineteen mules with thirty-eight empty leather oil containers. The twentieth mule was carrying two of the large jars filled to the brim with oil.

"Now listen to me carefully," whispered the captain cautiously. "When we get near the city gates, each one of you is to hide in one of the oil containers and to stay there with your weapons till I give you a signal. Leave the rest to me."

Soon it was night. A white moon sailed across the dark sky as the captain, disguised as a merchant, led the twenty heavily laden mules towards Ali Baba's house. In the bright moonlight it was easy to see and easy to count the houses. Before long he was hammering at the right door.

"Who is such a late visitor?" asked a voice from inside, and the captain replied, "I am a merchant from a foreign land. Be kind enough, sir, to permit me and my mules to spend a night with you, if this is possible. All the markets and lodging houses are closed at such a late hour."

Ali Baba opened the door and saw a stranger with his tired beasts. "I welcome you, brother," he said cordially. "Please make yourself at home here." And he led the crafty captain up the stairs while his servant attended to the mules.

What more could the captain want? The trusting Ali Baba suspected nothing. It never occurred to him to see in this polite merchant his vicious, blood-thirsty enemy, especially when his guest offered him the goods he had brought to sell in the city.

They ate, drank and made merry, and talked well into the night. Then Morgiana noticed that there was hardly any oil left in the lamp. She decided to fetch some, but it seemed there was not a drop left in the whole house. Then she remembered that the visiting merchant had offered olive oil to her master. She therefore picked up her jug and hastened to the yard. "Surely he will not mind if I help myself to a litre or two," she said to herself.

The oil containers were standing side by side near a high wall where Ali Baba's servant had put them.

The girl was about to open the first container, when she heard a whisper from inside. "Has the time come, captain?"

Any other servant would most probably have fainted with terror, but not the faithful Morgiana! In a flash she put two and two together, and realized it was not oil, but a thief who lurked in that bulging container. Calmly she replied in a deep voice, "Not yet, wait a little longer!"

She was greeted with the same question from inside the next container, and by the time she reached the end of the line, she had counted thirty-eight thieves in all.

Not until she came to the last two jars did she find the oil. It was then that she suddenly had an idea. She ran back on the kitchen, and came back with a large copper kettle, which she filled with oil and placed on a fire. She stacked a bundle of fine, dry wood under the kettle to make it come to the boil as quickly as possible. When it was sizzling and bubbling, she took the kettle back to the yard, and into each of the containers she poured enough boiling oil to kill the bandit inside.

Having done this, she returned to the house, and filled the oil lamp as if nothing had happened. Next she put on a beautiful dance dress made of rich brocade, which was fastened with a diamond-studded belt, from which hung a small dagger. Then she sought out Abdullah the servant, and said to him, "Take your drum, we are going into the dining hall to entertain our master and his guest."

Ali Baba was delighted at her thoughtfulness, and turning to his guest, said, "Look at my slave, dear sir. You will not find another to equal her charm and her skill in dancing. Her cleverness is exceptional too. After a good dinner it is only right that we should be entertained by her dance."

The captain nodded his head in agreement, but secretly he was seething with angry impatience. "If only Ali Baba would stop this unnecessary nonsense and go to bed," he thought. Then he could have his revenge. But he had no choice but to appear pleasant and bide his time.

Abdullah began to beat the drum and sing. Morgiana danced beautifully. She moved now fast, now slow, with grace and perfect rhythm, and her face was as fresh and lovely as spring blossom.

The dance came to an end. The girl took the drum from Abdullah and curtsied before Ali Baba, as if asking for payment. Her master gave her a dinar, and she turned then to his guest. The captain was about to take a coin from his purse, when, like a streak of lightning, Morgiana leapt to his side and thrust her sharp dagger into his heart. The robber gasped and fell lifeless to the ground.

"You wicked girl," shrieked Ali Baba. "What have you done? Do you want to ruin me? You'll pay for this deed with your life."

"Be calm, dear Master," the girl said quietly and fearlessly. "I killed him to save you. For this man is no ordinary merchant from some distant land, but the leader of the band of robbers you so much fear. Come, I will show you, and explain everything." And she led the stunned Ali Baba into the courtyard to the containers which held the bodies of the dead bandits. Then she told him everything from beginning to end, from the moment when the robbers had marked his house with the white cross.

Ali Baba knew then that Morgiana spoke the truth. Deeply moved by her loyalty towards him, he said, "How can I show my gratitude? You have now saved my life many times. Your devotion is such that I can never hope to repay you. I will give you your freedom; but that is not enough. I shall give you also my son as a husband, to care for you till the end of your days, for I love you both most dearly."

172

Morgiana and Ali Baba's handsome son were overjoyed to hear his decision, for they had always been fond of one another.

There was just one thing in this extraordinary tale which Ali Baba could not understand. He was quite sure there had been forty thieves in all, but only thirty-eight corpses had been found in the jars. What could have happened to the other two? Not knowing whether they were dead or alive, and perhaps waiting for their chance to revenge the deaths of their captain and comrades, he was loth to venture anywhere near the cave.

When a whole year had gone by without incident, he took courage and rode into the forest. There was no sign that anyone had visited the rock. All was quiet, and the entrance was thickly overgrown and almost hidden by bracken and bushes. Ali Baba knew then that no one had entered for a long time.

Thus reassured, he spoke the magic words, "Open, Sesame!" He went into the cave. Everything was as he had last seen it. It was plain that no one had touched the treasure since his last visit.

"The two missing robbers must also be dead," Ali Baba said to himself, gazing at the immense riches which now were his. But he was not grasping and greedy as Cassim had been. He filled only one bag with gold, and returned home, happy and contented.

From that day, until the day he died, he took from the treasure only what he needed. He was generous to the poor, was held in high respect by the rich and greatly loved by his family. And so his life passed in peace and happiness.

The secret of the cave he disclosed to no one, for he knew too well what tragedies human greed can bring.

Mohamed Lazybones

It so happened during the reign of the caliph Haroun al Raschid, the most renowned Prince of the Faithful, that his wife Zubaidah had a new crown made of red gold set with jewels.

The goldsmiths delivered such a work of art that it would have been difficult to find its equal. The crown sparkled with the dazzle of gold, rubies, pearls, emeralds, turquoises and topazes. But at the very top of the crown there was an empty space. A large diamond was to be placed there, but the goldsmiths had searched in vain throughout the kingdom. There

174

was not a diamond large enough or perfect enough to be found to set in the place of honour.

The caliph would not accept defeat so easily, and despatched messengers and merchants far and wide to search for a large and beautiful diamond. At last one day his vizier Jafar came to him with tidings which brought the first gleam of hope.

"I have been told that in the distant city of Basra," he said, "there lives a wealthy man who bears the strange name of Mohamed Lazybones. I have been told that his treasures are so immense that there must surely be a jewel amongst them of the right size and of a quality worthy of your wife's crown."

"I have never heard of this man," Haroun al Raschid remarked. "But I order you to go to him without further delay and to ask him to bring me such a jewel."

The vizier willingly obeyed the ruler's command, and soon was on his way to Basra. It was easy to find Mohamed Lazybone's home, for his was the most magnificent palace in that city.

Mohamed Lazybones received the vizier with all honour and insisted that his guest must first dine with him and rest before they both made the journey to Baghdad. Jafar gasped when he saw the lavish table set before him, and exclaimed, "I have never seen such a feast even in the palace of our caliph, the ruler of all believers!"

But it was not just the feast which was worthy of Jafar's admiration, but everything around him, from the soft cushions embroidered with gold and set with jewels, to the grand marble bath house. Jafar had not dreamed that things of such beauty and exquisite taste existed as those which filled every room of the palace.

Mohamed Lazybones only smiled at his guest's enthusiastic remarks. And at the close of day, when the weary traveller had retired, he ordered that large chests be filled with his most priceless jewels, in readiness for his journey next morning to the caliph of Baghdad.

Haroun al Raschid was agog with impatience. Would the mysterious and wealthy stranger bring the jewel? How had he acquired such riches? These and similar questions plagued his mind and creased his brow in a frown, until at last he saw the procession entering the palace gates.

And then Mohamed Lazybones was presenting himself to the caliph, greeting him with the utmost respect, and ordering his slaves to bring forward the chests full of rich gifts.

As the chests were opened one after the other, the caliph gazed in wonder at the beautiful brocades and gold ornaments studded with diamonds, pearls, emeralds and sapphires, any one of which would have fitted into the space in his wife's crown.

"Oh Prince of the Faithful," exclaimed Mohamed Lazybones, "each of these jewels is a royal stone; I am but a common man, not worthy of such precious rarities. Therefore it is my pleasure to offer them to you as a gift."

With these words any doubts the caliph had about Mohamed Lazybones disappeared. He took the rich visitor to his heart and showered him with kindness.

He waited till the evening, when darkness had fallen and the time was right for story telling, before he said: "You have a most uncommon name, and most uncommon wealth, Mohamed Lazybones. I am aware that your

father left you no fortune, for he was but a poor man. Explain to me how you came by your name and your riches!"

"I shall be only too pleased to tell you my story," answered Mohamed Lazybones, "for it is indeed a most unusual tale and should amuse you.

"It is true that my father left me no property; he was a poor man, a simple assistant in the bath house. But this did not stop me from being all through my childhood and youth the laziest being on this earth. My mother had to feed me and dress me and help me to get about. Believe it or not I was too lazy to get up myself and move out of the hot sunshine into the shade.

"This went on till I was fifteen years old, for then my father died and we became very poor. My mother worked like a slave and pinched and saved wherever she could. But it was no good — my laziness soon brought us to such a state that we lost the roof over our heads and in the end all we had left were five pieces of silver.

"One day we heard that the sheikh Muzaffar, who was a most noble fellow who loved the poor, was about to sail to China. My unhappy mother, who did not know which way to turn, came to me and said, 'You must rise, Mohamed Lazybones, and take these five dirhams to the sheikh, and ask him to barter with them in the foreign land. Perhaps he will buy wisely and make a profit for you, and perhaps it will be the beginning of a better life...'

"But I was too lazy to rise and turned away from her onto my side. At this my mother grew very angry, and swore by Allah that if I did not do as she asked for once she would let me die of hunger and thirst.

"I knew she meant what she said, and as I had no wish to meet such a fate, I sighed and said, 'Very well then. Bring me my clothes and put them on, then put on my shoes.'

"She put on my last shirt and my last pair of shoes, and then helped me to stand up. I was so lazy and so fat that I could not walk on my own, but had to be supported and helped along to the port. By the time we got there, the rumour had spread that Mohamed Lazybones was out for the very first time, and it reached the sheikh Muzaffar's ears long before I did.

"He was therefore already waiting to greet me, and when I handed him the money and spoke my request, he said, 'You have made a wise decision, Mohamed Lazybones, for money should be wisely used to make more money, and not wasted on idle spending. That way it can bring respect, honour, and beauty to your door...'

"As we bade each other goodbye, his parting words were firmly

imprinted on my memory, and I have tried to live accordingly ever since.

"The sheikh, in the meantime, sailed in the company of merchants to China, and there they carried out successful business deals. Not until they were back at sea and had sailed for three days on their return voyage, did the sheikh remember my five silver pieces.

"Angry at his forgetfulness, he wanted to turn the ship eastwards again, but the merchants persuaded him not to do so, and each offered instead a sum of money to make up for my lost profits.

"This was the beginning of my wealth.

"But sheikh Muzaffar was still looking for an opportunity to keep his promise to me. Soon the chance came. On a certain island where the ship anchored to take a supply of food and water, he saw a monkey seller, surrounded by a group of monkeys. One of these had a patchy, mangy coat and a sad face, and the other monkeys kept teasing it, nipping and biting it whenever their master was not looking.

"The kind sheikh was sorry for the pitiful creature, and asked the monkey seller, 'How much do you want for that poor specimen?'

"The man replied, 'Just five silver pieces. You wouldn't get another for such a low price.'

'Done!' said the sheikh, taking the monkey and handing over the money.

"Soon the ship was sailing across the sea again with the monkey on board. Later it anchored off another island which was rich in pearls. Everyone on deck discarded their clothes and dived into the sea, and no one came up empty-handed. The monkey watched for a time from its perch on the mast, then it too dived with a splash into the water. Everybody cried out, thinking it would surely drown, but to their amazement up it came again, clutching the largest pearls of all. And honest Muzaffar added these to my property.

"But this is not the end of the tale. When they came to the island of Zanzibar, the ship was attacked and all on board were imprisoned by the black cannibals, who occupied that island. Their king announced to the unfortunate men that next day at sunrise they would be put to death and then devoured.

"The prisoners' last night was slipping away, when suddenly my monkey appeared before sheikh Muzaffar.

'Help us, please, untie our bonds,' Muzaffar whispered.

'We shall all reward you with a thousand dinars each.'

"The monkey nodded its head in agreement, then quickly loosened the ropes which held them till they were all free. Before the eastern sky had paled the ship was gliding at full sail away from this dangerous place.

"After that the voyage passed peacefully enough and soon the ship docked in the port of Basra once again. I was summoned to go and see Muzaffar for the second time.

"This time my mother did not have to help me to my feet. I stumbled along on my own, helped by curiosity and hope. The riches which were waiting for me surpassed all my expectations.

"Not only did sheikh Muzaffar give me everything he owed to the last coin, but he also thanked me for entrusting him with the five silver pieces, for with them he had bought the monkey which had saved his life and the lives of all the other merchants. Afterwards he gave me good advice. He told me to buy a shop and some land and farms and to work hard and enrich myself.

"I acted on his advice, for he was the kindest, most honourable man I knew, and though I was stuck with the name of Mohamed Lazybones, I no longer lived up to the name, but worked hard from morning till night.

"My businesses prospered, not only through my own efforts, but also thanks to the monkey.

"Every day it brought me, I do not know from where, a purse containing a thousand dinars.

"One evening, instead of leaving me, the monkey stayed by my side and addressed me in a human tongue, 'Mohamed Lazybones, the time has come for me to tell you about myself...'

"I was utterly terrified, and wanted to take to my heels. But the monkey stopped me. 'Do not fear me, and do not run away. I am a marid of the genies, who once sinned so much against the human race, that I was ordered to bring happiness to a human being to atone for my sins. You are the one I chose, but my task is coming to an end. All that remains for me to do is to find for you a wife you will honour and love.'

'Do you know of such a maiden?' I asked with growing excitement.

'Yes, I do. She is as beautiful as the moon; she is like a fresh flower kissed by the dew. She is well born. She is altogether outstanding.'

'Who can she be?' I asked, now full of interest.

'She is the daughter of our most noble citizen, the caliph himself...'

'But I am no suitable match for her,' I objected.

'She is as noble as you are rich,' the monkey continued.

'Though the caliph is a descendant of the Prophet, I am sure he will be pleased to marry his high birth to your property. Go to him and ask for his daughter.'

"The marid was right. He offered one thousand dinars to the caliph and the wedding agreement was signed. The wedding itself would take place ten days later.

"On the eve of the wedding the monkey came to me and said,

'Mohamed, tomorrow you will attain your greatest happiness and then my punishment will at last be over. But to allow me to return to my own kind, I have one small request to make...'

'Just name it, and it is done,' I assured the monkey without the slightest hesitation.

'When you enter your bride's chamber, you will see a closet by the door. Inside the closet sits a white cockerel. You are to slit its throat, and make sure it bleeds to death.'

"I did not dream the words could have an evil meaning, for the monkey had brought me nothing but good. So the following morning I dressed in the most magnificent robe and hastened to the caliph's palace.

"I gasped before the loveliness of my bride and had to force myself to remember the marid's request. At last I was alone in the chamber. I opened the closet door.

"The white cockerel was perched inside. I slit its throat as I was told to do, but at the same moment it seemed as if the sky fell down and hit the earth. The whole world spun and shuddered and thundered and I was lost in terrifying darkness, till mercifully I fell into unconsciousness.

182

"I do not know how long I lay there, but when at last I was able to see. I found the caliph standing over me, lamenting bitterly, 'Why did you do that?' he cried. 'Instead of a happy wedding, only sorrow awaits you now. That cockerel in the closet was my daughter's talisman which kept her safe from the wicked marid! For many years he has desired to have her in his power, and as he was unable to touch the white cockerel with his own unclean hands, he sent you to do the black deed for him!'

"Oh, how I cursed myself for being so gullible and trusting, but this brought me no relief. The caliph banished me from his palace and I, full of grief, turned towards the desert.

"I cannot tell you where I wandered, how many nights turned into days. But I remember well that suddenly one night a shadow rose before me against the starlit sky, and spoke in a soothing voice, 'Do not despair! Not only goodness, but evil too has its enemies. I am one of the faithful genies, a believer, and I am here to offer you help. It was I who gave your bride the cockerel talisman to keep her safe from the wicked marid. The evil creature has taken her to the distant city of brass where he holds her prisoner. I can take you there this night, if you so desire.'

"How could I refuse such an offer!

"And so we flew with breathtaking speed towards the east, and when at last the marid slowed down and descended, we had arrived by the city walls.

'These walls are made of brass, and this is where I must leave you,' the genie said. 'You yourself must find the way to reach your bride and then to free her...'

"With that he was gone, never to appear again.

"I stood in front of the brass walls, looking for an entrance. But there was not a gate, not a door, not a hole in sight. There was just one spot in the foundations through which a narrow, but deep stream flowed.

"I dived into the water, swimming with the current under the surface for as long as I could. When I emerged again, I could hardly believe my eyes. Lo and behold! I was in a beautiful garden and on the bank of the stream my bride was reclining on a seat.

"The moment she saw me, she cried out in delight and surprise. Then becoming calm, she told me how both of us could be saved. 'The proud. conceited marid in a thoughtless moment showed me where he keeps his lucky talisman. It is hidden in the head of a pillar in the centre of this garden. If you take it and set it alight, then throw in a little musk, all the little spirits which the marid has in his power will obey your command.'

"I arose at once and climbed the pillar, and did exactly as she had bidden me. In a trice I was surrounded by a swarm of little spirits, each of them saying, 'At your service, master!' So I said to them, 'Place the wicked marid in irons, and collect all the treasures of the city of brass!'

"Oh, Prince of the Faithful! The spirits worked quickly and soon collected all the treasures of the brass city. The marid, who had turned again into a mangy monkey with a patchy coat, could only stare and spit with hate and anger. Without his talisman he was helpless.

"Afterwards the spirits transported my wife and myself and all the riches of the city of brass to Basra. Once there, remembering all that had happened, I broke into a thousand fragments the talisman with my own hand. Before my eyes the monkey who had followed us shrank and became a pile of ashes which were blown away forever by the wind."

"You deserve your wealth, Mohamed Lazybones," said the caliph after a moment's silence. "For you knew how to stretch out your hand towards the grace of God, and not a single grain of Allah's gifts has slipped through your fingers."

The Cunning Dalila

The reign of Haroun al Raschid did not only benefit those who were brave and wise, but also those who by their wit and cunning succeeded in gaining the caliph's favour.

In the city of Baghdad one such man, by the name of Hasan Shumad, was appointed Haroun's own vizier. The caliph was a far-sighted man, who was well aware that this vizier was a clever trickster and that his shrewdness could be turned to his own advantage.

Not so pleased by far were the other tricksters, swindlers and plotters, forgers and cheaters of the city. In the first place they were afraid of the new vizier, and in the second they envied him greatly.

But in the whole of Baghdad there was not a heart so filled with envy as that of a certain old woman called cunning Dalila. Evening after evening her spiteful tongue wagged on and on spitting out biting words of hate. "That rogue of a fellow Shumad," she would say to her daughter Zainaba, "sits there all snug and smug in the caliph's palace, collecting at least a thousand dinars per month, whilst the likes of us haven't two coins to rub together..."

Such bitter thoughts did not give her a moment's peace, till at last she could bear it no longer. "This can't go on," she decided. "I must do something about it. Tomorrow all Baghdad will see what I can do! Just wait! I'll get a thousand dinars in just one day!"

"It is about time we brought our name to the caliph's notice again," Zainaba added, nodding her agreement. "My father used to be a noted leader of this city, but now that he is dead, no one wants to know us."

The following morning Dalila dressed herself in the flowing white robe of a holy woman. Her face masked by a veil, she went out into the streets, calling in a loud voice to Allah, as if she were in a trance.

Passers-by moved out of her path and showed their respect. She came at last to an imposing house which was the home of the emir, a wealthy town dignitary. Dalila's sharp eyes immediately noticed a young woman standing by the window. She was clad in a magnificent robe adorned with exquisite jewels which must have been worth at least a thousand dinars. So she stepped nearer still, shouting the name of the Almighty at the top of her voice.

She had judged that face by the window well. After a time the porter opened the front door, and said, "Oh, divine apostle of our Maker, my mistress asks you to visit her."

The old woman pretended not to notice him, so he was forced to repeat the request several times over. At last, shaking herself out of her supposed trance, she followed him in. Once inside, a maid took over, and led her to the emir's wife. Dalila recognized her straight away as the lady by the window.

"Hear me out, for I am a poor unfortunate woman," began the emir's wife in a sad voice. "Only you can help me, for it seems you were ordained to come to this house..."

186

"I will do so gladly," Dalila replied gravely, while her mind was calculating how much the robe and the jewels would fetch. "All that is necessary is that you tell me what is troubling you. God is all merciful."

"I have been the wife of the emir for many years now, yet we are still without a son or daughter. And now my husband has declared that if I do not bear him a child by the end of the year, he will drive me out of his house and wed another."

"He won't have to wait as long as that. Come with me to my house, for this very day I have acquired the herbs which will help you."

Together they left the emir's house, Dalila a few steps in front, eager to find a suitable place in which to carry out her intentions. They zig-zagged through the streets, till the old woman noticed a dye shop.

"Wait here for a moment. I must send my slave to fetch food and drink," she said, pointing to the dyer who was dozing in front of his shop. Hurrying to his side, she woke him up with a whisper, "Listen dyer: good people have sent me to you, because you have a large house and a kind heart. That damsel you see waiting over there is my daughter, who is soon to be married. This is why I have engaged builders to extend and improve our house. But now we have to move out for two months. Tell me you will rent us three of your rooms for that length of time."

The dyer scrutinized Dalila's robe and the young woman nearby. "I just happen to have three rooms you can use," he said, and handed over three keys.

"Now please go and buy us some food," Dalila ordered. "I shall look after your shop."

The moment the dyer had disappeared round the corner, both the women went in. Dalila opened the door of the first room. "Here you must discard your jewellery and robe," she said to the emir's wife. When this was done, she unlocked the second door.

"In this room you must wait, while I prepare a bath containing the magic herbs," she said and disappeared behind the third door. From here she passed to the back stairway, then crept round and re-entered the first room to collect the robe and the jewellery. Carrying these she walked brazenly into the street. But instead of being content with her theft, she was thinking up more mischief. A donkey-seller, who was strolling by with his beast, gave her an idea.

"My good man," she addressed him. "You are just the fellow I want. My son, the dyer, is in financial difficulties, and I am hastening to take away some of the most valuable items before the court officials arrive to confiscate everything. I'll give you a dinar if you lend me your donkey, and while you are waiting for my return, you might as well go into the dye shop and help yourself to whatever is of use to you. But I want you to break up the dye tubs with an axe, so that everyone will know my son has gone bankrupt and that he cannot repay his debts."

Naturally the donkey-seller was only too pleased to oblige. He lent the donkey to the old woman and ran towards the dye shop.

Dalila calmly walked home, where between bursts of spiteful laughter, she told Zainaba all she had been up to during the day. "Mother dear, I fear you'd better not show your face in the streets," said her daughter. She was right.

For what a commotion there was at the dye shop! The dyer caught the donkey-seller red-handed breaking up his shop. The noise of the quarrel brought the half-clothed emir's wife from her room. They shouted abuse and accused one another till it seemed half of Baghdad was crowded round the dye shop, and the commander of the guards at last appeared to bring order.

But they did not find cunning Dalila. She ventured out into the streets the very next day, this time disguised as a servant. She was determined to finish what she had set out to do. And once again it was not long before she saw and seized her opportunity.

In the house of the city's chief merchant preparations were going on for the wedding of his eldest daughter. His wife therefore entrusted her youngest child to the care of a most reliable maid, while she herself supervised the wedding arrangements.

The maid was playing with the little boy in front of the house when Dalila called,

"I can see I have come at the right time," she spoke in a pleasant voice. "Hurry and tell your mistress that I am here to help," and she passed the maid a dinar.

"But who will look after the boy?" the maid objected, her fingers at the same time closing round the coin.

"Don't worry, I will attend to him. Don't waste time, but go," said the old woman.

The minute the maid had disappeared, Dalila, making quite sure she was unobserved, seized the child and ran as fast as she could round the nearest corner.

188

"Thanks be to Allah for man's stupidity," she gasped breathlessly delighted at her success. "Now they will all see what I am capable of!"

Her destination was a certain little goldsmith's shop which belonged to a Jew named Adhra, who was renowned in the whole city for being the greatest miser and the worst cheat.

"I have hurried here to you," Dalila began, still breathless. "You must surely know that my mistress, the wife of the chief merchant, is today preparing the wedding of her eldest daughter. She has sent me to you for a selection of hair combs and jewellery to the value of about a thousand dinars. I am to leave her little boy here as a guarantee that she herself will come to you later."

Adhra the Jew was beside himself with delight, for he had not made such a good sale for quite some time. He chose beautiful combs and brooches, bracelets for wrists and ankles, necklaces and a jewelled belt. The old woman took them all supposedly to her mistress, leaving the child in the shop. Soon she was lost among the crowds in the market.

She was just in time, for in the meantime the chief merchant had discovered what she had done, and he himself was searching for her. Asking everyone he met, he scoured the streets, and when finally he arrived at the goldsmith's shop, he met not only the swindled Jew, but also the swindled dyer, the donkey-seller, the emir and the commander of the guards. They all put their heads together and decided that each one would go after Dalila in his own way, and the commander of the guards would send ten men to find her.

But there were so many old women in that city! That day they did not find her, and she would most probably have evaded them the next day too, if it had not been for the donkey-seller. Even in the crowded street he recognized her at once.

"You wicked old hag!" he cried, gripping her arm. "Give me back my donkey!"

"How glad I am to meet you, my son," Dalila replied meekly. "That donkey of yours has earned you so much money, that I have had to hide him under bulging sacks over there at the barber's," she said, pointing to the barber shop which belonged to Magrihan Masud. "Stay here a moment while I run over and tell him that he is to give you the donkey, sacks and all..."

The donkey-seller obeyed. "I shall make money after all," he thought, "and the Almighty might turn a blind eye on the rest..."

But he did not know Dalila.

"Listen, Masud," she cried to the barber, as soon as she stepped over the threshold. "I know you are good at pulling out teeth. In fact I've been told you're better at it than anyone in Baghdad. My son over there is going mad with the pain in his two wisdom teeth. The poor fellow is so crazed he doesn't know what he is talking about — he keeps jabbering away about some donkey. Here's a dinar for your trouble, take him and pull out the cause of it all, and may Allah reward you."

Masur pocketed the money and stepped into the street, while the old woman hurried off as fast as she could go.

"My donkey, my donkey," the donkey-seller was wailing, when he saw the barber approach without the beast.

"Stop crying," Masud said reassuringly. "Your donkey is waiting for you inside." With that he pulled him into his shop. Next moment he gave him such a blow on the head, that the dazed donkey-seller sank into the barber's seat. In a trice his hands and even his feet had been bound, and

while he screamed and yelled for help, two good, sound wisdom teeth were extracted.

"I must be more careful," Dalila muttered to herself as once again she made her way through the city streets. But this time her fortune changed. She was recognized and caught by the guards and taken, her hands tied, to the commander's house, where the emir, the dyer, the donkey-seller, the Jew, the barber and the goldsmith were waiting. As it was already dark, they made her lie on the bare floor, while they reclined on soft mattresses and cushions. As soon as the sun came up, they decided, they would take her to the judge.

Dalila pretended to be fast asleep. The guards, completely taken in, began to nod, doze and finally fall asleep. Dalila's six victims were also soon asleep. Only the donkey-seller tossed restlessly, his gums throbbing with pain.

The old woman had been waiting for this. Noiselessly she left the room and entered the chamber where the commander's wife was resting. Kissing her hand, she said, "I am looking for your husband. Is he already asleep?"

"Yes, he is. What do you want?"

"I have brought him six slaves, which he purchased from my husband for a thousand dinars. And I have also come to collect the money, for we are leaving the city early tomorrow morning."

"Show me the slaves and I will pay the price agreed upon," said the commander's wife.

The cunning Dalila then boldly led the woman into the room she herself had left only a moment earlier. It was to her advantage that the room was so dark that the wife of the commander could only make out the sleeping guards by their uniforms.

"My husband has acted wisely," she said. "We need large, strong white slaves such as these." And without hesitation she counted out the thousand dinars and gave them to the scheming old woman.

It is easy to imagine how next day Dalila and Zainaba roared with laughter, and how the respectable Baghdad citizens complained at being hoodwinked once again. Realizing at last they themselves would never outsmart Dalila, they decided to take their complaint to the caliph.

Haroun al Raschid listened carefully to their case against Dalila and then turned to his viziers and said, "Which one of you should I make responsible for that old woman?"

"Let me be the chosen one, oh Prince of the Faithful," said Hasan Shumad. "But let me take to her your handkerchief of mercy. Then I guarantee Dalila will return everything."

"She is lucky to have you to speak on her behalf," the caliph remarked, and commanding him to bring her to the palace, he dismissed the vizier.

Hasan Shumad knew where the old woman lived, and he went at once to her house.

"Cunning Dalila!" he cried, standing under her window. "Look out at me. I have brought you the caliph's handkerchief as a sign that he will pardon you for all the tricks you have played on those six citizens. But you must return with me to the palace for a hearing."

192

Presently the old woman came out of her house and meekly permitted herself to be led to the caliph.

"Why did you practise such trickery and why did you choose to turn the whole city upside down?" asked Haroun al Raschid sternly. "Why, all Baghdad is talking about your deceit and lies and these poor fellows have lost property through your misdeeds!" He pointed at the six plaintiffs.

"I did not desire their possessions, oh Prince of the Believers," Dalila replied in her defence. "But up to now everyone in Baghdad has talked of nothing else but the clever trickery of your noted vizier, Hasan Shumad. I wanted to try my hand at something similar, and to prove to you I was equally capable. Thus I too would gain your favour and be held in high esteem by all..."

"You have certainly shown yourself to be a mistress of deceit," agreed the caliph. "And as I have given my word to pardon you, you can also ask a favour of me."

"If this is so, let me have the position of housekeeper with a salary of a thousand dinars a month, which is what my late husband used to bring home when he was a highly respected citizen of the city."

Haroun al Raschid granted her request. Then all the victims of her tricks took what was rightly theirs, except for the donkey-seller, who of course could not have his teeth back. But Dalila compensated him amply, and made sure too that the dyer had enough money in his pocket to refurnish his shop with brand new equipment. And so they all returned to their homes satisfied and contented.

Dalila and Zainaba settled down again and lived happily for some time, respected by everyone in Baghdad. Their reputation spread far and wide, as far in fact as distant Cairo, where the rumours reached the ears of Ali, the greatest and most notorious clown and trickster of that city.

It was said that just as Dalila outshone everyone in shrewdness and craftiness, so her daughter outshone everyone in loveliness. "It would be a very good idea to marry such a girl," Ali thought to himself. And because he was never slow in putting thought into action, it was not long before he was on his way to Baghdad.

On the very day Ali reached the city, Dalila brought home a star chart, and together with Zainaba they read what awaited them in the future. And lo, the name Ali of Cairo appeared on the chart. And it was written that he would outdo them with his wit, and that good luck favoured him more than it favoured them.

"We must seek out this stranger and put him to the test," Dalila laughed, little knowing that he was already standing outside their door. Next moment he was being announced by their maid.

"The rumour about your fame and your daughter's beauty, dear lady, has flown all the way to Cairo," Ali began. "This is why I have come here to beg you for Zainaba's hand, for there would not be a better pair than the daughter of Dalila and Ali of Cairo."

"Not so fast, young man," the old woman remarked, stopping his flow of words. "Whoever wishes to marry my daughter must first prove that he is worthy of such an honour. If you fulfill the task I shall give you, we will write out your marriage agreement."

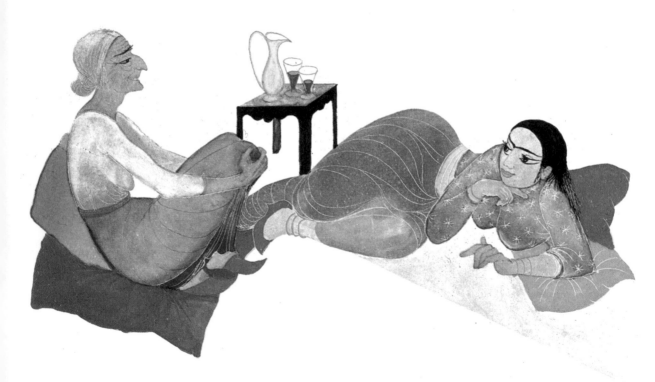

"Please tell me what I am to do," Ali asked.

"Listen carefully," said Dalila. "My Uncle Zuraik is a miserly old hoarder, who would stop at nothing to get a single dinar. He has a shop in the market where he fries fish, and over the door of that shop he always hangs his bag with two thousand golden pieces. You are to get that bag and take it to the vizier Hasan. He will justly decide whether you have carried out the task well."

"But do not think," Dalila continued, "that it will be easy. Zuraik uses that bag of gold as bait to lure people to his shop and to profit from them. You see there are little bells and little brass rings all round that money, so that as soon as anyone touches the bag, it starts to quiver and tinkle and chime. Then my crafty uncle pounces on the offender and he has to buy his freedom."

"I am the chief trickster of Cairo," Ali boasted. "It is a simple task for me to carry out. Tomorrow I shall return and we shall seal the marriage contract. That pouch of gold will be Zainaba's dowry."

However, it soon became obvious that this particular task would not be so simple even for the notorious Cairo jester.

First of all Ali disguised himself in woman's clothing and tried to lure Zuraik's attention away from the doorway. But he failed and was caught red-handed.

Then Ali met a travelling entertainer who was a snake charmer, and he borrowed his pipe and his sack of snakes. The miser feared serpents, so Ali let them out of the sack. But even then Zuraik did not lose his presence of mind, and caught the would-be thief.

"I will have to steal that money from his house," Ali decided in the end, so just before Zuraik locked his shop, he ran ahead to his house and hid in the cellar.

"I couldn't leave the money in the shop," the old miser muttered to his wife, frowning angrily. "Some crafty thief would be sure to break in and take it." And he proceeded to tell his wife what had happened that day.

Down in the cellar Ali waited patiently. At last all was quiet in the house, and he crept out of hiding. There was the pouch, right by Zuraik's bed. Ali grabbed it and ran down the stairs as noiselessly as a shadow, as quickly as an arrow in flight. Even so the old man woke up.

"Catch him, catch him," he cried, but his wife, who also was awake by then, snapped back, "You catch him! And if you come back without the money, I shan't open the door!"

Ali was already outside, running for all he was worth, but he was near enough to hear these words.

"I must run in a circle," he thought. "Otherwise I will lead that Zuraik straight to the vizier Hasan." So quickly he zig-zagged through the streets.

But the old miser had learned where Ali was heading, so instead of following him, he went straight to the vizier's house. Fortune favoured him. The doors were unlocked. He entered, locking the door behind him, and waited.

Not long afterwards the panting Ali appeared. As soon as he knocked on the door, he heard from inside the words: "Did you bring it?"

"Yes, I have it here, chief of the viziers! The task is completed!"

"Let me see then," said Zuraik, and pushed his hand through the little side window by the entrance. "Then I will unlock the door."

The unsuspecting Ali, who had no reason to think he was not speaking to the vizier, handed over the gold. He waited and waited for the door to open. He hammered on it with his fists, till at last someone came. But by then Zuraik had long been gone by the back door...

"What now," moaned the miserable jester, when he had finished relating to Hasan Shumad all that had happened.

"There is plenty of time left till morning... And I am sure that Zuraik has not gone to bed. He will be celebrating with his neighbours that he has outwitted you," said the vizier.

Now Ali remembered something... and he raced back to Zuraik's house. He knew it would be locked, but he himself had left a window open, just in case it was needed.

He slipped inside, put on the first piece of woman's clothing he could find, then started to go through all the rooms, searching for some handy container. A basket! That was just what he wanted. Excited and hopeful again, he hid with the basket under a window by the entrance.

Zuraik was approaching, singing merrily. Before he had the chance of knocking on the door, Ali leant out of the window, and disguising his voice to match the female clothes, he whispered, "Have you got it? If not, I am not letting you in!"

"I have the pouch here with me, so let me in," Zuraik replied, thinking that he was speaking to his wife.

"I want to make quite sure. I cannot believe you were capable of outsmarting the greatest trickster in Cairo," Ali said, still whispering so that

196

the old man would not recognize his voice. "I am going to put my basket out of this window. Place the pouch in it, so that I can inspect it."

And the old man was fooled in the very same way he had fooled Ali only an hour before. Perhaps he was still standing by his front door in the morning, when Ali and Dalila were making out the marriage contract.

Let it be known, however, the pouch of gold truly belonged to Zainaba and was meant for her dowry. For old Uncle Zuraik was keeping it just for her; but he wished to make sure that the pouch and his niece would only fall into the hands of a man who was worthy of both. By succeeding in outwitting him, Ali was the worthy man.

What a Drop of Honey Caused

There was a hunter who loved and valued his dog above all else and took him each day into the desert or to the mountains to hunt.

It happened one day that as they were wandering among the rocks they came upon a cave. Inside they found a deep hollow filled with bees' honey.

The hunter scooped it into the leather bag which he had with him, slung it over his shoulder and hastened to a nearby village to sell the honey.

He knew the local shopkeeper, so he went straight to him, and it did not take long for them to agree on a price.

But as the shopkeeper was ladling out the honey from the bag, one drop of it spilled on the floor. In a trice a swarm of flies settled on it, but before they could suck it up, passing sparrows dived upon the flies. This caught the attention of the shopkeeper's favourite cat. Like lightning she pounced on such an easy prey. But before she had a chance to have a taste, the hunter's dog sprang, bit and killed her. The sight of his dead pet made the shopkeeper lose his temper. He kicked the dog so hard that it too died instantly. Did the hunter stay calm? His fury was so great that he pulled out his knife and killed the shopkeeper. But as his anger subsided, he came to his senses, and, terrified at what he had done, he took to his heels and fled.

Soon the shopkeeper's neighbours discovered the bodies and guessed what had happened. They raised the alarm and presently every villager was armed and on the march against the hunter's village. But as if this was not enough — the two villages were in different provinces and each of these belonged to a different ruler. After the attack on the hunter's village, the ruler declared war on the ruler of the shopkeeper's village. The armies met in a fierce and mighty battle. Soldiers were killed in their thousands and by then only the Almighty knew that it had all been caused by a single drop of honey...

Sinbad the Sailor

The wondrous city of Baghdad is renowned for its magnificent minarets and palaces, its glorious, ancient history, and also within the city walls there lived men whose adventures were as colourful, rare, and wondrous as the city herself.

Sinbad the sailor was one such man. Though he had never been skilled in the art of sailing, he acquired his name because his desire to sail the mighty seas had led him to regions where till then no human foot had trodden, and from which no living soul had ever returned. But destiny smiled on Sinbad, and allowed him to live through and relate the undreamed of adventures and experiences of his voyages in the seven seas.

Sinbad was but a young lad when his father died, leaving him his fortune. Instead of making the most of his wealth, in no time at all the reckless Sinbad had squandered most of the money and property. His so-called friends were only too eager to help him spend money and join him in his riotous living.

One day Sinbad realized he would be face to face with poverty if he did not mend his ways, and he resolved to abandon his thoughtless behaviour. He sold all that was left to the highest bidder, and, pocketing the money, joined some merchants, who were about to embark on a ship to trade in foreign lands. It was then, as he sailed from the port of Basra that he first fell under the spell of the mysterious seas and the excitement of the unknown.

The journey proved to be filled with unexpected surprises. Just to watch the varied and many-coloured shoals of fish in the water, or to sight islands, large and small, flat and treeless, hilly or rich in plants and flowers, whose people spoke in unfamiliar tongues and were quite unlike the people Sinbad had up till then known — all this excited and gave him pleasure.

One day the ship approached a little island, as vividly green as the ocean in which it lay. Beautiful birds danced and flapped their wings by the shore, gazing at the intruders with curiosity.

The captain ordered the anchor to be cast, and allowed the passengers and the crew to go ashore. Everyone was glad to stand again on firm ground. But alas it soon proved to be not so firm! Some of the men lit a fire to cook over and suddenly the peaceful green island erupted like a volcano! It trembled and shook and spat and fumed, and then, as if struck by an earthquake, it began to slide and disappear into the depths of the sea!

"Get aboard, get aboard!" the captain cried frantically. "That is no island, but an enormous whale which dislikes having a fire lit on its back."

Those near the ship were lucky enough to escape from the terrible, foaming whirlpool. But Sinbad felt himself being mercilessly pulled down by the surging waters. His arms threshed about helplessly, till suddenly his fingers touched a wooden object. It was a barrel and thankfully he gripped it hard. Sinbad managed to climb on top of it and so he drifted with the waves till the surface grew calm.

His eyes searched the waters around him, then filled with tears — there was not a sign of the ship, his fellow merchants, the crew... He was all alone, at the mercy of the vast ocean. It was then that he lost consciousness.

Who knows how many hours went by as the barrel and Sinbad floated on waves, but when his eyes opened at last, he found that he had been cast by the sea onto an island. The barrel was now firmly wedged in a rocky hollow at the base of a rugged cliff which towered above him.

Exhausted and bruised he rose to his feet and looked round. "Where was he and was there any life on this island?" he wondered. By now the sun was high in the sky as he dragged his feeble body forward, looking for something to stay his hunger. At last he found some berries to eat and also a spring of fresh water to quench his thirst.

With renewed strength he ventured further inland.

Suddenly he came upon two men who, they said, were the subjects of King Mirchan. How surprised they were to hear his strange tale, but they were friendly and told Sinbad to follow them, and they would present him to their king.

Mirchan too was friendly. He made Sinbad welcome, lavished gifts upon him and ordered his servant to see to his every need and comfort. He even appointed him supervisor of the port.

Sinbad was grateful for all these kindnesses, but his heart yearned for his native Baghdad. Wistfully he watched ship after ship sail into the harbour, but none were bound for his beloved city. At last, one day a familiar vessel hove into view. The youth could scarcely believe his eyes, but one look at the captain told him that he had not been mistaken. Yes, it was the same ship, the same captain, the same crew and the same merchants that he had sailed with to that fateful green "island".

It did not take Sinbad long to convince the captain that he had not drowned in the turbulent seas, as everyone had thought — but was here before him, alive and well and eager to return to his native land.

King Mirchan was sorry to lose his new friend so soon, but pleased to see him so happy at the prospect of returning home, he did not try to force him to stay. They bade each other farewell, and Sinbad boarded his ship, laden with all the gifts the king had showered upon him.

The winds being favourable, it was not long before the ship sailed into the port of Basra. Sinbad returned home to Baghdad, once again rich enough to buy a fine house, hire good servants, and enjoy the pleasures of life with his friends and family.

The story of his adventure soon spread through the city and from that time he was called by everyone Sinbad the Sailor.

The Second Voyage

Sinbad soon changed his mind about staying quietly in Baghdad. He was much too restless. He wanted to return to the life of a trading merchant that he had enjoyed on his first voyage. Above all he wanted to travel again to strange and distant lands. It was not long therefore before his steps led him back to Basra.

He could not resist the sight of the ships, their bright sails flapping in the warm breeze, their crews busily loading and unloading cargoes. So Sinbad

again joined a group of merchants who were about to set sail. Equipping himself with goods and merchandise, which he thought would bring him rich profit, he was soon back on deck, sailing from city to city, from island to island. And he succeeded in selling and bartering his wares at a high profit.

One day the ship landed at an island where the vegetation was lush, where beautiful fruit trees grew and green meadows and clear brooks were everywhere. But there was not a man, or a beast to be seen.

Sinbad went ashore with the others, but after he had his fill of the fruit, and had eaten the food he had brought from the ship, he fell asleep in the shade of a tree. When he awoke, he found to his horror that the ship had gone — he had been left behind!

Sinbad was in despair, and angry with himself for not staying in safety at home. But it was useless to spend time regretting his decision. Here he was, quite alone. He must bestir himself and at the same time try to avoid all dangers...

Gathering his courage, he climbed a tree and looked around in all directions. In the distance he could just make out a large, dome-like shape, and he decided to go closer and investigate.

"What a strange thing!" he thought as he came nearer. "It looks like an enormous white bowl." He went forward to touch it. Its surface felt as smooth as silk.

He counted fully one hundred steps as he walked round it, but there was no door and no way of climbing on top. Puzzled and curious, he wondered what this mysterious structure could be. He did not have to wait long for an answer!

As soon as the sun began to set, an immense black cloud appeared in the sky and everything was suddenly cloaked in darkness. But it was no cloud above, but the wings of a giant bird! And this bird came to rest on the smooth white dome...

Suddenly Sinbad knew what he was looking at. The giant bird was no other than Roc and the white dome was its egg! Sinbad recalled having heard sailors and wanderers speak of it with awe. They said that Roc's newly hatched chicken would be capable of devouring a whole elephant.

The sight of the enormous bird gave him an idea: Taking the turban from his head, Sinbad unwound it and tied himself to the bird's foot, which was as thick as a tree trunk. And so he waited all night, in fear and excitement. What would happen to him when daylight came?

When the sky reddened with the morning light, the bird, screeching horribly, rose from the egg. He did not notice Sinbad clinging to his foot.

Roc climbed higher and higher into the clouds, whilst the ocean waves rolled below, and Sinbad shook with fear of being discovered.

At last the bird began to descend, so rapidly that Sinbad almost lost his senses. They were diving towards a large island and aiming for a deep rocky valley. Once down, Sinbad quickly untied his turban from the bird's foot and hid behind a nearby boulder. Fortunately for Sinbad, Roc's attention was attracted by an enormous, hissing snake. This was quickly captured in the bird's claws and lost in his beak. Thereupon Roc rose again and disappeared in the clouds.

"I think I would have been better off had I stayed on the island with the giant egg," Sinbad said to himself, gazing at the desolate landscape around him. The valley was so grey, so bare, there was not a green leaf to be seen or the brightness of a single flower. And there was no sign of a path which would lead him from this hollow.

Sinbad rose to his feet and walked about aimlessly, wondering what to do. It was then he looked down at the stones which were strewn on the ground. They seemed uncommonly shiny, unusually bright. Yes, they were no ordinary stones, but precious ones — diamonds in a variety of shapes and sizes!

Sinbad, excited at first, then began to tremble. How many times had he heard the travelling traders mention with fear Snake Valley, which was occupied and guarded by thousands of poisonous serpents? He remembered them saying that no living man could hope to escape except at the time when the bird Roc came to catch snakes to feed his young.

"I must get away from here quickly," Sinbad thought. "I have escaped from danger before and I shall again." Stuffing several handfuls of the jewels inside his shirt, he turned towards a steep bank which might offer a way of escape.

As he went, he could hear the snakes slithering behind him, hissing menacingly. Glancing back, it seemed as if the whole valley was a mass of gleaming black waves. It was alive with the dark, moving bodies. There were snakes as gigantic as trees, there were small snakes which moved as fast as arrows, and all, large and small, were pursuing him, their green eyes aflame.

His strength nearly gone, Sinbad dug his fingers into the rock and climbed upwards in a frantic effort to escape. At last he reached the summit, and exhausted, he sank to the ground. Foiled by the height and steepness of the cliff, his pursuers could not follow and he heard the thud of their bodies as they fell back into the valley.

All at once Sinbad realized that he was no longer alone. Looking up, he saw the friendly faces of a band of merchants, who were eyeing him with curiosity. He sighed with relief and proceeded to tell them his story. He showed them the diamonds, offering to share the stones with them. But the kind men refused. Their hearts were not filled with envy, for there was not a man among them who would have cared to share Sinbad's adventure in the valley of the snakes.

"We are your friends and we will help you," they assured him. "Our ship is anchored nearby, and we shall take you with us."

Sinbad wept with happiness. How thankful he was to leave Snake Valley behind him for ever!

Eventually he reached Baghdad richer still at the end of his second voyage. Thanks to the diamonds he could afford to be generous to the poor and the needy, and himself live in luxury with his family and friends.

The Third Voyage

It was not long before Sinbad grew tired of his unadventurous life in Baghdad and started to crave new excitement and new travels to distant lands. Forgetting the dangers and the hardships, he was soon buying merchandise for his third journey.

At first all went well. He sailed with other merchants from Basra, touching at many ports and doing profitable business. But one day his ship was caught in a terrible storm which struck the vessel with full force, breaking her masts and steering wheel and driving her, helpless, towards an island.

The passengers were relieved to see its shores, but the captain cried, "We are doomed, for this island is inhabited by dreaded savages! They are no bigger than monkeys, but they attack in swarms like flies and are equally numerous! We must not resist them or try to defend ourselves. If we kill just one of these creatures, they will all turn upon us and destroy us."

Everyone on board was terrified, for even as he spoke, the captain's words were proving true. The dwarf savages, covered all over with bright

206

red hair, were swimming round the ship, climbing up the sides, taking down the sails and cutting the cable with such nimble movements, that one could have easily mistaken them for monkeys. They shouted to the dazed crew and passengers in a language no one understood, but their meaning was clear. They wanted them all to abandon the ship.

What else could the men do? Even the mountainous waves and the unknown island were preferable to being left at the mercy of these terrible monkey-creatures...

Fortunately most of the crew and passengers managed to swim safely ashore. After refreshing themselves with herbs and fruit which grew near the shore, they wandered off deeper into the island, and finally came to a magnificent, enormous building, surrounded by a high wall with a gate of ebony with double doors. They were open wide, as if in welcome.

They entered, and found themselves in a large courtyard, with roasting spits and huge cooking pots on one side and a heap of human bones on the other! Shocked and horrified, they trembled at this sight. Weary and in despair at their plight, they sank to the ground.

All of a sudden the earth trembled, and out into the courtyard stepped a fearsome black giant as big as a palm tree. As he walked his footsteps were deafening. He had but one eye, and that in the middle of his forehead where it glowed evily like a red flame. Sharp fangs protruded from his ugly mouth which was as deep as a well and equally wide. The repulsive giant had an upper lip which was split, and looked like a camel's, while the lower lip hung down, limp and swollen to his chest. His floppy, hairy ears were like an elephant's, and the talons on his fingers were like vulture's claws.

The sight of this monster struck terror into the hearts of everyone: indeed many fainted with sheer fright.

The monster sat down on an enormous bench in the porch and stared at the men intently with his evil, frightful eye.

But worse was to come: the monster rose suddenly and started to walk towards the men. Out shot his hand and Sinbad was gripped by the throat. Holding him high he examined Sinbad carefully like a butcher preparing for the kill.

Luckily Sinbad was too lean for his liking, so he was put aside, as were all his thinner comrades. From the plumper ones he selected the captain, who was most certainly the fattest. The monster ran a spear through the body of the unfortunate captain and soon he was being roasted on a spit over a fire, then eaten till there was nothing left but the bones. His feast over, the giant rolled onto the bench and soon his snores were thundering through the courtyard.

Those who were spared from this terrible fate could not rest or sleep, but passed the night in awful dread, wondering when their turn would come...

Their fears were justified. They could not escape, and as the days went by the monster devoured them one by one, according to their size and weight. It seemed none of them would escape being roasted on the spit or boiled in the cooking pot.

But at last Sinbad thought of a plan. "Comrades," he said, "do not lose heart. While he sleeps during the day, we will build several rafts and hide them. When darkness comes, we will try to make the giant harmless. If we do not succeed, we must reach our rafts and put out to sea. If we do, we can bide our time, and wait for some ship to come by and take us off this fatal island."

All that day they busied themselves building small rafts. And in the evening, as they were forced to watch yet another comrade disappear into the monster's mouth, their moment of revenge drew near. Once he had drifted into his noisy sleep, all the men who remained lifted the iron roasting spit which was still red hot from the fire, and with all their might pushed its burning point into the giant's eye.

Blinded, the monster rose to his feet with a fearful cry. He groped for the men with his hands, but as he could not see, they avoided him easily and made their way towards the rafts, while the monster staggered into the open, howling in agony.

The men thought they were safe from him now, but on glancing back, they saw to their terror that the giant was pursuing them, supported by two other identical monsters... Without hesitation they took to the rafts and rowed for their lives. But the giants were hot on their heels and arming themselves with large rocks, they threw these at the rafts, sinking all but one.

Sinbad's raft was the only one to escape, and he and his two comrades were the only men to survive. All the others drowned. They were now at the mercy of the sea currents, the winds and the waves. But destiny was kind. The raft was driven to a small island where there was fresh spring water and fruit to eat. Their hunger and thirst satisfied, Sinbad's two friends settled down to sleep on the sand, but Sinbad chose to climb into the crown of a tall tree.

In the middle of the night he was awakened by piercing screams. Looking down, he was horrified to see his companions being attacked by a giant snake. He could do nothing to help as he watched them being devoured by this creature whose body was as thick as a stout branch.

All night Sinbad crouched in terror in the tree. The snake made several attempts to reach him — he could hear it hissing and slithering near the tree. But fortunately for Sinbad a ring of thorny bushes grew round its base which kept him safe for the time being.

He did not think he would live to see the dawn — but at last the sky turned pink and with the first light he could see, Allah be praised, the white sails of a ship. Shouting with all his might and waving his arms, he finally caught the crew's attention. Slithering down from the tree, he evaded the snake and raced to the water's edge.

And strange to relate, the ship which rescued Sinbad was the very one which left him years before on the deserted island and sailed away with his merchandise. The captain was an honest man and had not touched any of Sinbad's property.

And so Sinbad returned to Baghdad richer than when he had left and soon had put the sufferings and the dangers he had faced behind him.

The Fourth Voyage

This time Sinbad was content to stay at home for some time, but at last once again he was filled with longing to sail the endless oceans and experience new adventures. His restlessness soon drove him back to the port with a fresh supply of goods, and before long he was off on his fourth voyage.

It was in Persia he met and joined a group of traders, and together they sailed across the seas, stopping at the islands, the strange cities, everywhere successfully enlarging their fortunes.

But one day a violent storm arose, which tossed the ship wildly, ripping her sails and bringing down her masts. Many of the crew and passengers disappeared forever in the swirling, mountainous waves. It seemed they were all doomed and would perish in the foaming, hungry ocean, when the ship struck some underwater rocks, and battered and broken, it began to sink.

Sinbad and a few other lucky men escaped with their lives. The current carried them to a nearby island and they staggered ashore, weak with exhaustion, hunger and thirst.

They had barely survived one disaster, and already another calamity was awaiting them. Before they could go off in search of food and fresh water, they found themselves surrounded by wild looking, naked savages, and led to their chief. He ordered food to be brought, and straight away some very strange looking and strange smelling dishes were placed before them.

Sinbad's companions ate hungrily, but Sinbad, suspicious of the unfamiliar smells, tasted only a little. He found it so disagreeable that he spat it out at once. He was glad, when he noticed that the food was having strange effects on his companions.

All the men appeared to be enjoying what they were eating more and more. Faster and faster they emptied the dishes, which were immediately replaced with full ones by the savages, smiling strangely. In the end the ravenous men almost tore the dishes from their hands.

Suddenly the awful truth hit Sinbad. The food was poisoned, it had robbed the men of their reason, and they were now staring at him with a vacant expression, like beasts, understanding nothing.

The chief of the savages laughed derisively. "Enough now!" he said. "After today we'll put them out to grass, and when they are fattened up, we shall hold a feast!"

Sinbad looked on helplessly as his friends bleated like sheep and crawled about on all fours. Those cannibals, having dulled their minds with poison, were now preparing for the kill!

His fears proved, alas, too true. Sinbad was the only one who kept his life and sanity, for he only pretended to eat and to drink. No longer could he make his companions understand anything he said. They were quite demented, and he himself had grown so weak and so thin, that he knew he had to escape before he became too ill to try.

One day, when their guard had dozed off, Sinbad seized the opportunity. He got to his feet and ran to some nearby bushes. Once past them he found a narrow track which he followed as quickly as his weakness allowed, not pausing till it grew dark. And even then, after a short rest, he journeyed on through the night, determined to put as many miles as possible between himself and the awful savages...

Sinbad wandered on for many days, living only on coconuts and not meeting a living soul. How great was his joy when he climbed a hill and saw the sea glistening on the other side. Several boats were anchored in the harbour; there were people about too, busily picking peppers, and they were not in the least like the cannibals he had left behind!

Sinbad therefore approached them without fear and told them all that had happened. They had heard of the terrible man-eating savages, and they were amazed that he had managed to keep his sanity and life.

They insisted that Sinbad must travel with them to their own island to meet their king. The ruler, when Sinbad had been presented, was only too pleased to listen to the tales of his adventures. He made the sailor welcome and comfortable, for he had taken an instant liking to him.

After so much suffering it seemed that good fortune was smiling on him at last. Sinbad applied his knowledge and ability in trading and before long became a highly respected and a very wealthy citizen of the community.

One day Sinbad noticed that no rider used a saddle, a bridle or stirrups on his horse — not even the king. So he asked, "My Lord, why do you tire yourself by riding without a saddle?"

"I have never heard of such a thing as a saddle," replied the king. So when Sinbad realized that no one on that island knew such a thing existed, he asked for leather and wool for stuffing the saddle to be brought. A leather craftsman and a locksmith came to him and under his guidance, a saddle, a pair of stirrups and a bridle were completed by the end of that day. When all was ready he fitted a quiet little mare with all the equipment and explained to the king and to all the onlookers how to use it.

Everyone loved riding in the saddle — particularly the king. And because this new invention had increased Sinbad's popularity and reputation, and because the king had taken him to his heart, he not only rewarded him most handsomely for his services, but also gave him his daughter in marriage.

But Sinbad was fated not to enjoy for long his newly found happiness by the side of his beautiful wife. Before their first year together had ended, the princess fell ill and died.

"It is my sad duty to inform you, my dear son-in-law, that you too must say farewell to this world," said the king solemnly, after expressing his deepest sympathy. "For it is our custom that whenever one spouse dies, the other too must enter the grave. Accordingly the living husband is buried with his deceased wife, and the living wife with her deceased husband. In this way they remain together for ever, beyond this life, beyond this world..."

Sinbad pleaded and protested, pointing out that such a cruel custom should surely not be applied to foreigners, but it was all to no avail. Three days after his wife's death he was led to the burial place on the cliff near the sea. A large boulder was lifted, showing an entrance to a deep hole resembling a well, and Sinbad, still pleading and protesting loudly, was lowered down with his wife's coffin and a jug of water and seven loaves of bread. The opening was then covered again with the boulder, and Sinbad found himself in complete darkness and absolute silence, surrounded only by human corpses.

The sailor was filled with despair and terror, and reproached himself bitterly for not having been satisfied with his riches and for embarking on this fateful journey. There was no one to answer his cries, no one to help.

Hour followed hour, day followed day, but the only way he could measure time was by the dwindling of his meagre rations of bread and water. Sinbad did his best to make his provisions last as long as possible, but the moment he so dreaded was eventually upon him. He had eaten the very last crumb, drunk the very last drop...

After that he spent his time in prayer, turning his thoughts to Allah. As if in answer, a miracle occurred. The rocks around him began to tremble and crack, then crumble with a deafening roar. Soon all was quiet again and still, but now Sinbad could see a glimmer of light — bright, clear daylight which, after the small earthquake, was now shining into this horrible, frightening grave.

Without glancing back he hastened to the opening, ignoring the sharp rocks which tore his hands and feet. He did not stop till he had squeezed through into the open, and then only to shield his eyes from the glare of the blazing sun and to thank Allah for saving him from such a horrible death.

Before him lay the shore, and, as luck would have it, a ship was anchored very near the rock he stood upon. Sinbad ran towards the sea, and easily

persuaded the ship's captain to take him on board. Soon the island lay far behind them.

Eventually Sinbad reached Baghdad again, thankful to return to his normal, happy life.

The Fifth Voyage

When the misery and distress of his last trip faded in Sinbad's memory, he was seized with the urge to travel once more. This time he used some of his riches to have his own ship built. He chose a captain and crew to man her, and traders to accompany him with their wares. And so his fifth voyage began.

How thrilling it was to be back on board, how magnificent was the wide sparkling sea, how tempting were the unknown green shores!

It so happened that the need for drinking water forced the ship to stop at a desolate island where there was no sign of human life. Sinbad was loth to disembark, so he stayed on deck watching the others row to the shore.

Soon their excited cries caught his attention. Near the water's edge they had come upon an enormous white globe, which could not be anything else but the egg of the bird Roc. Ignoring Sinbad's shouts of warning, the men used their hammers and axes to smash the shell and kill the young bird which was about to hatch. They then carved its young, tender flesh for their dinner.

"May Allah have mercy upon us," Sinbad cried. "That egg belonged to the giant bird Roc and he is sure to seek his revenge! Most certainly we shall all pay dearly for your thoughtless deed! Hurry back on board; we must leave this place."

The moment everyone was back, the ship sailed away as fast as the wind would take it from the dangerous island. Soon it was only a speck on the horizon.

The sea was calm, the waves were gently caressing the ship, the sky was clear, and everyone began to feel safe. Suddenly a thick, dark cloud blotted out the bright sun. Not just Roc, but both parents of the young bird the sailors had killed were circling above, croaking dreadfully. In their claws they held an enormous boulder. Then suddenly they stopped their flight right over the deck and let the rock drop. The aim was good, and the

vessel broke in half as easily as if it had been made of plywood. Those who did not die when the rock struck, were thrown into the deep and drowned. Only Sinbad was destined by Allah to be saved by swimming to a nearby island.

He was not to know that this beautiful island which looked like paradise, tempting him with its fruit-laden trees and bushes, colourful singing birds and clear sparkling brooks, was also the home of the wicked Old Man of the Sea...

Just as the thirsty Sinbad was scooping water from a brook, he saw a very old man, wearing nothing but a loin cloth, in which he was wrapped from head to foot.

"Please help me, my good fellow," he cried in a weak voice to Sinbad. "My legs no longer serve me, and I should so like to refresh myself with a drink!"

Sinbad was only too pleased to help the old man who looked so withered and frail. He took him on his back, but all at once he felt the old man's legs digging into his hips like irons.

"I have fooled you, stranger, and now you will suffer!" the old man cried, his voice now strong and evil. "I can force you to carry me wherever I wish, and you shall never be free of me, not till death liberates you…"

The terrified Sinbad did his best to shake the evil old man off his back, but the more he tried, the harder his tormentor dug his heels into him, beating him at the same time in his ribs and stomach. Sinbad was in such pain that sparks danced before his eyes. But he had to go on, obeying the old man's every whim, always to the accompaniment of curses and blows. He kept his legs round Sinbad's neck even through the night, and treated him as if he were his horse.

When several days had passed, Sinbad found a large dried gourd and thought of a way to ease his suffering. He cleaned it out and filled the inside with the juice of some grapes, which grew in abundance on the island. He left it to ferment in the hot sun, and eventually it turned into wine. The effect of the wine was strong and brought him release and strength at least for an hour or two.

At first the old man just watched Sinbad drinking from the pumpkin, noting how merry it made him, so much so that he even sang and danced while he carried him along. Eventually curiosity got the better of him: he demanded to try it too, and emptied the pumpkin in one gulp.

As he was not used to drinking, the wine went straight to his head. He began to shout and throw his arms about, till he was completely overcome and senseless. Sinbad felt him growing as limp as an empty sack on his back.

He had been hoping and waiting for this. He shook himself free of the troublesome burden and the old man collapsed in a helpless heap on the grass. Sinbad ran for his life from that awful place.

He did not stop until he was back on the shore, scanning the horizon for a sign of some ship. But he had to wait several days before a vessel finally appeared and anchored off the island.

Once safely on board, Sinbad related to the captain and the crew his nightmarish adventures with the evil old man.

"You were the victim of the Old Man of the Sea," said the captain, eyeing the sailor with admiration. "No one else has ever managed to escape from his clutches. You are the very first."

A day or two later the ship anchored in the harbour of a strange city completely surrounded by a high wall. Sinbad noticed a group of people busily throwing small stones at some monkeys which were leaping and

208

the water, he begged the Almighty, "In the name of my newly born, may it please your Lord to grant me a living which is easy and adequate."

But it seemed his wishes went unheard, for his net remained empty. He threw it back into the sea again and again, but no matter what he did, luck did not smile upon him and still it remained empty. Downhearted, he turned at last towards home, wondering how it was possible for God to allow his child to be without food — for after all, it was God's duty to feed anyone that he created; that went without saying.

Poor Abdallah was plagued with such thoughts, till he arrived in the town and came to a baker's shop. There he could not help stopping, for he smelt the enticing smell of freshly baked bread. Then he continued on his way, his head bent, for he did not have a single copper in his pocket.

The baker, however, who happened also to be called Abdallah, noticed his behaviour and called, "Abdallah Fisherman, don't go away! Why didn't you take your loaf as always?"

"I cannot do so, Abdallah Baker," replied the fisherman and proceeded to admit with some bitterness how badly he had fared that day and how hard it was for him to go home empty-handed.

The baker did not hesitate. Not only did he give his unfortunate friend a loaf of bread, he gave him five dirhams as well to buy other food.

"Please take it, for you need the money. When your catch is a good one there will be time enough to repay me."

The fisherman showered the baker with words of thanks, but the latter interrupted. "Why should'nt I help? After all, I too carry the name of Abdallah. Abdallah, the servant of God..."

The fisherman went home, his face creased in a happy smile, and told his wife what had happened.

Early next morning he left to catch as many fish as he could, eager to repay the debt.

The first time he threw his net into the water, his effort proved useless. Abdallah had no luck the second time either, and as the day progressed, his despair grew. He was beginning to feel sorry that he had not given up fishing a long time ago, and concentrated instead on some other work which might have given him an easier living.

While he was thus immersed in his thoughts, he was pulling his net out of the water. Suddenly it struck, just as if a heavy object had been caught in it.

Straight away he was all attention, all excitement. He pulled and pulled with all his might till the veins stood out on his hands and arms. And there was his catch on dry land at last. But what a catch it was! The swollen carcase of an ass, which spread such a foul smell all around, that Abdallah swiftly freed his net and hurried away from that spot.

Once again he fell victim to despair and vowed that this would be the last time he would try his luck. It was almost night when at last he decided to pull his net out of the sea.

Once more it seemed that the net was exceptionally heavy, far heavier in fact than before. He grappled with it, breathing heavily, tugging and heaving, until at last it lay on the shore. To his amazement his catch turned out to be a strange green being, rather like a man, except that it had an enormous fish tail instead of legs.

234

Abdallah was so terrified that he dropped his net and was about to take to his heels. After all, what else could that creature be but one of the evil genies who had been imprisoned during Sulaiman's reign in its prison bottle, so that it could do no harm!

But the horrific creature called, "Don't go away, Abdallah Fisherman, I have no intention of harming you!"

What was the poor man to do? He returned, though unwillingly, and the green one continued, "I am not a genie, I am one of the believers, like yourself, but I happen to live under water. And I also happen to be called Abdallah."

"What were you doing in my net?" asked the fisherman, gathering his courage.

"My sovereign king has ordered me to bring him fresh fruit. I cannot go and pick it myself — in no time at all the wind would dry out my skin and I would perish for lack of water. That is why I chose you, hoping to strike a bargain: If you are willing to bring me a basket filled with fresh fruit tomorrow and all the following days, I will in return fill it for you with corals, pearls and other precious stones."

The fisherman could hardly believe his ears. He never dreamed he could lay his hands on such riches...

"Let us seal our bargain with the opening words of the Koran, Abdallah of the Sea," he gasped, wanting to safeguard his unexpected good fortune.

So they both recited the first verses of the Koran and thus sealed their bargain. Afterwards Abdallah of the Sea started to slide back into the water.

"Tomorrow we shall meet again here. Come and bring the fruit. All you have to do is say, 'I am here, Abdallah of the Sea,' and I shall swim to the surface."

Then he was gone and all that remained were a few ripples and waves, and the fisherman was alone with his still empty fishing net. Everything that had happened seemed to him to be but a dream...

All the same he hurried unashamed this time to Abdallah Baker to get some bread, and to tell him his unbelievable story.

The baker was only too pleased to learn of his friend's change of fortune, and not only gave him bread on account again, but also made sure that the fisherman had the freshest and the choicest fruit to be found in the town to give to Abdallah of the Sea.

And when night was gone and daylight lit the sky, the excited fisherman was already standing with a full basket on the seashore, calling to the waves, "I am here, Abdallah of the Sea!"

The waves murmured and parted, just as if someone was running a comb through them, and Abdallah of the Sea appeared.

"I am here! If you have carried out your part of our agreement, I too shall keep my promise," he said. When the fisherman had handed him the basket of fruit, he dived under the surface again.

He was not gone for long. In a minute or two he was back, and what he brought took the fisherman's breath away — glittering pearls, corals and other gems, the like of which had never, he was sure, been seen by a human being. And all that was to be his daily reward!

The fisherman, dazed and dazzled with his good fortune, hardly knew how he got back to town. His wife, however, was shrewd enough to know how paupers such as they should treat such wealth. It would not do for them to disclose it to the powerful men of this world. It was better to keep it a secret and to use it only slowly and gradually to trade with to their advantage. His friend the baker was the only man the fisherman told of his good luck, and he was amply rewarded for his past kindnesses with several handfuls of the riches from the sea. But this generosity led to the whole matter reaching the ears of the sultan and to the consequences of this.

For the baker, unlike the fisherman's wife, did not keep his gems hidden away at home, but took them to the market. As soon as he showed them to the jewel merchants, the guards were upon him, while the chief merchant shouted orders that he should be beaten and bound, for he must surely be a thief! How else could a poor man as he come by such jewels? They were probably the property of the sultan's wife, and he must be the thieving baker who stole them.

No one but the sultanna could prove whether or not there had been a theft. As soon as she looked at them she said to her husband, "Any one of these precious jewels would do justice to a queen, but there is no royal gem finished by a human hand to equal them. That is why I do not see anything here which rightfully belongs to my personal treasure."

After hearing her words the sultan grew angry with the envious, unjust men of the market, and he spoke kindly to the terrified baker and gladly listened to his tale.

And because he too was blessed with the name of the servant of God — Abdallah the King — he gave him his favourite daughter for a wife, and promoted him to the rank of Vizier of the Left. As for the fisherman, he was

236

given the status of Vizier of the Right, and his wise wife became the First
Lady Vizier...

Now good fortune it seemed was smiling on all the Abdallahs on the
earth, and the agreement made between the fisherman and Abdallah
of the Sea, was fulfilled daily.

Some time later, when Abdallah Fisherman met his green friend on the
shore as usual, Abdallah of the Sea asked him to place a gift at Mohamed's
tomb in his name.

The fisherman was only too happy to agree, but how could he — an
ordinary mortal, step into the depths of the sea to fetch it?

But Abdallah of the Sea explained. "The underwater dwellers have no
protection against the dangers of air, but this ointment will give you all the
protection you need against the sea."

And he showed him a strange yellow cream which had a pungent fishy
smell.

237

"This ointment comes from the liver of the largest fish of the sea," Abdallah of the Sea continued. "If you rub it into your skin, you will come to no harm."

The fisherman did as he was told and lo and behold — the surface of the water parted to let him in, and he was able to walk upon the sea bed as if it was dry. He followed Abdallah of the Sea and the water did him no harm. And he saw so many rare, extraordinary things that one would need many books to describe them.

He saw submerged cities whose inhabitants wore no clothing. He saw fish building houses for them. He saw women and maidens who were more beautiful than any on earth. But without exception, though they were similar to people on earth, all the underwater inhabitants had fish tails instead of legs.

As Abdallah with his two legs looked so very different, they laughed at him till tears rolled down their cheeks and some moments passed before they were composed enough to lead him to their sea king.

At first he too roared with laughter at the sight of the bewildered visitor, then he rewarded him handsomely and retired.

After a long journey they at last came to the house of Abdallah of the Sea, where everyone present was making merry. Abdallah Fisherman had never in his life seen such jollification.

"You must surely be celebrating a wedding," he remarked to his friend, but Abdallah of the Sea shook his head: "That is not so; someone close to them has just died."

"But surely it is not proper to sing and laugh at a funeral," the fisherman objected. "At home people cry with grief and pain."

At hearing those words Abdallah of the Sea turned on the fisherman and cried in rage as if he was the greatest heathen, "Does not the Almighty determine your destiny? Is it not he who puts you on earth? Are you not happy when it is time for your spirit to return to him? No, I can see now that you are not worthy of taking my gift and greetings to the tomb of the Prophet, nor worthy of our continued friendship!"

Having spoken so harshly, Abdallah of the Sea led the fisherman back to land, and then he sank back into the waves never to reappear. His mortal brother called and called to him from the sea shore, but it was in vain; of the four Abdallahs only three remained.

238

But only Abdallah the King, so old and so wise, realized that the friendship between Abdallah Fisherman and Abdallah of the Sea had been severed forever. For even laughter and tears can be important matters of true faith.

How Abu Kasim Came to Be the Supreme Judge

Nobody knows today whether Abu Kasim was first or last in the queue when wisdom was being accorded to mortals. But it is well known that the ruler of all believers, caliph Haroun al Raschid, kept him well under his protection, though many times he could not help laughing at him.

You can judge for yourselves:

One day the strangest court action came before the caliph; it was about "nothing". It happened that a merchant from Basra was selling slaves to another merchant. After much bartering they agreed on a price, but then the first merchant could not resist making one last attempt to raise his profit. "What will you add to it?" he asked.

"Nothing," answered the buyer. But that was not the end of the matter.

"Give me that 'nothing' then," the merchant from Basra insisted. "If you don't, we shall go to the judge!"

But even the judge did not know how "nothing" should be paid. And that is why the quarrel eventually came before the caliph.

Haroun al Raschid listened to both the seller and the buyer, then he declared, "This indeed is a very strange case. Whoever solves it justly will be named the Supreme Judge."

Many learned men, influential men and wealthy men attempted to settle the quarrel, but they did not succeed. Then one day an ordinary, simple drummer called Abu Kasim, renowned as a tight-fisted skintflint, came to see the ruler.

"Bring me a basin and water," he said to the caliph, and when the basin stood before him, he took the merchant from Basra by his hand.

"Clench your fist," he commanded. When this was done, he plunged the merchant's fist into the water. After a time he took it out and said, "Open your hand. What have you got in it?"

"Nothing," answered the mystified merchant.

"In that case, how dare you ask for another 'nothing' then?" stormed the drummer. "Away with you from this court, or you'll be asked to pay a fine!"

The merchant ran for his life. In a few moments he was lost in a cloud of dust. And the caliph laughed and laughed till tears streamed down his face and he fell back exhausted with mirth.

And that is how Abu Kasim came to be appointed Supreme Judge.

Abu Kasim's Babouche

Though Abu Kasim no longer beat his drums, but sat instead side by side with the highest and wealthiest dignitaries, he did not shed his old bad habits, and if anything he was a greater miser than before.

He was in fact so tight-fisted that he would almost prefer to starve than pay for his food, and would wait for others to invite him to dine. He looked more like a beggar than a judge, for his clothes were in tatters, and he even grudged the copper needed to take a bath. Needless to say people avoided him when they could, both because of his meanness and because of his unpleasant smell.

"One of these days your greed will be your downfall," Haroun al Raschid would say. But even he did not realize how soon his words were to come true.

The cause of it all was Abu Kasim's old babouche.

For some time this miserly supreme judge had only one left of his pair of slippers, but he refused to part company with it. Yet there were his filthy toes sticking out of the many holes, and thanks to it, he became more than ever the laughing stock of the town. He went on refusing to get rid of the slipper, however, until it kept falling off his foot and tripping him up. Then regretfully he decided the time had come to throw it away.

He made this decision while standing on the terrace of his house, and without thinking, he threw the babouche onto his neighbour's roof. What had he done! As it landed it made a hole in the roof, the babouche fell

through, there was a sound of broken glass, falling flasks, breaking bottles and then a great crash.

Abu Kasim hardly had time to get off the terrace when his furious neighbour, who was a chemist, rushed to his house, waving the offending slipper in his hand. He screamed at him at the top of his voice, "You won't judge yourself out of this one, Kasim. In fact I'll make sure you pay for every bit of the damage!"

There was no help for it. The judge was forced to go and view the damage himself. The slipper had fallen on a shelf which was filled with expensive bottles of scent. They had fallen over and rolled onto the shelf below, and their contents had of course spilled everywhere. So it went on till finally some of the bottles had fallen to the floor where a most valuable vase was standing, but stood no longer. It was shattered. And from that

flood on the floor rose the strong aroma of amber, musk, aloe and roses. It was so strong that Abu Kasim's head spun.

"What a disaster, what a mess!" he wailed. But there was nothing else he could do but pay for the damage. He had to count out there and then a thousand dinars in all.

After that there was only one thought in his mind — how to be rid of that babouche. So when darkness fell he took a spade and a rake, having decided that the only thing to do was to bury the offending slipper. He found what he thought was a suitable place near the mosque. Here the soil was soft, so he buried the slipper at least one metre deep.

"Now it will worry me no more," he muttered, pleased with himself, as he dragged himself homeward towards morning.

But his joy was short-lived. Two or three days later the town guards came for him.

"Is this your babouche?" the commander asked sternly, gazing with distaste at the repulsive object which was the cause of a fresh disaster.

"It is," the judge admitted grudgingly.

"In that case you'll get a hundred blows of the stick and you'll pay a fine of ten thousand dinars! That slipper blocked the canals of this town and the water had overflowed."

Abu Kasim almost fainted. What a scandal, what punishment!

He did not regain his composure till several months later. Only then was he able to think in a clear, sensible fashion.

"I must get rid of that babouche, come what may. I've already lost half of my property and if things go on this way, I'll soon become a beggar," he said to himself. "But I daren't decide myself what is to be done. Let someone else advise me." That was the conclusion he finally reached.

Having so decided, he went straightaway to see the barber who was famed for his good sense and humour.

When the barber had listened to all his lamentations, he offered the following advice. "Cut that troublesome slipper into four pieces. Take each piece to a different spot and hide it well. Just make sure it is away from the town!"

Abu Kasim thanked him gratefully — he would do that, and then surely all his troubles would be over.

For the next three days he left the town and each time he left one quarter of the slipper in a different spot. On the fourth day he wandered into some fields near a river and for a long time he was unable to find a suitable hiding place. It was already growing dark when he noticed a pile of bricks, so he placed the fourth piece of the babouche amongst them.

For some time afterwards Abu Kasim waited, still worried that something else might happen. But nothing did. At last he began to think that bad luck had stopped pursuing him. But he was wrong. When winter arrived, the rain filled the irrigation canals; only the biggest field right by the river remained dry. All the people were most surprised at this and the unfortunate ones who owned that field were beside themselves with despair. Without water that field would remain barren!

Then was only one thing left to do — dig up all the installations and clean them all out. So they set to work and soon they found the cause of the trouble: that last fragment of the fated slipper had blocked the hollow bricks!

The furious farmers ran towards the judge's house, cursing him loudly and brandishing their sticks. But Abu Kasim did not wait. Realizing what he had done, he fled from the town, as far away as he was able, leaving his house and all his possesions behind. He was only glad to have kept his own life, and he never showed his face in that town again.

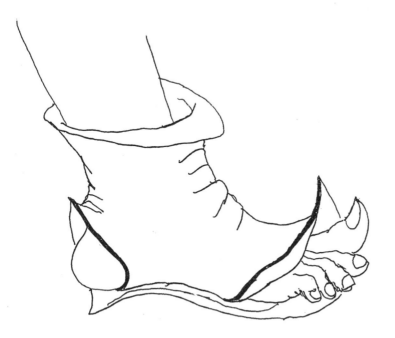

Prince Ahmed and the Fairy Pari Banu

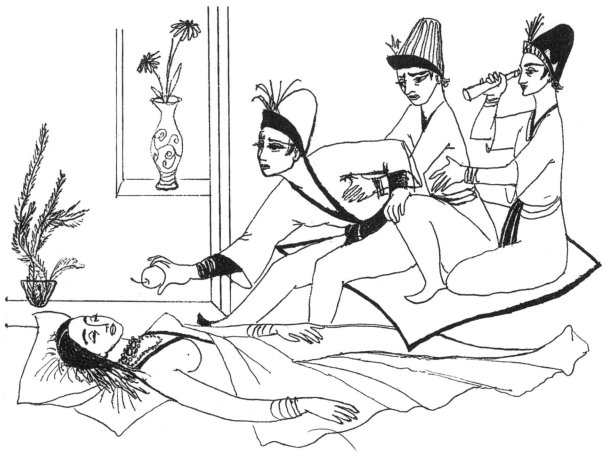

Three handsome sons had the Indian king; Husein the eldest, Ali the second, and Ahmed the youngest. The boys grew from babyhood in friendship and affection. Their greatest love and joy was their cousin Nur en Nahar, who spent all her days with them, for her father, the king's younger brother, died tragically soon after his daughter's birth.

The princess was not only sweet, kind and beautiful. Her uncle made sure she attended the very best school, so that when she was grown up, there was no one her equal in the whole wide world.

How could anyone be surprised then that her three cousins fell desperately in love with her, and each and every one desired her for his wife?

The king understood well what was going on in his sons' minds, so he called them to his side one day and said, "My dear sons! Nur en Nahar deserves your love, but as only one of you can have her for a wife, I shall give her to the one who proves himself to be most worthy of her."

"What should we do?" Husein asked impatiently.

"You will all go out into the world. Whoever brings the most valuable and the rarest gift by the end of the year will win the princess."

All three at once agreed to their father's wise suggestion, and before very long they were speeding on horseback through the palace gates, accompanied by servants and advisers.

They travelled along the same path all day long, but as the sun began to set, they reached a crossroads: one path led to the right, the second to the left and the third went straight on.

"It is time to bid each other goodbye," Husein said. "It would be best for us all to meet here again in exactly one year's time."

Then each one chose a direction to follow.

The eldest prince chose the path to the right, for he well remembered that it was supposed to lead to the far away Bishanghar Land on the banks of the Indian Ocean, and he knew it to be a region rich in the rarest merchandise.

He travelled many days and many weeks along caravan trails till at last he reached the capital of Bishanghar.

All he had heard proved to be true; what he saw in the bazaars and stalls in the streets was beyond all expectations. Such a variety of jewels, beautiful materials, exquisite flowers — all of which took his breath away. He walked tirelessly from stall to stall, yet he was unable to find a suitable gift for the princess.

His steps led him to a dark little back alley, where suddenly an old wrinkled man appeared before him. He held in his hands a vividly coloured carpet.

"I will sell, I will sell, it is the only one of its kind!" he cried, offering it to the prince.

"How much do you want for it?" Husein asked, more out of curiosity than an intention to buy.

"Three thousand gold pieces," answered the seller, lowering his voice. "But this is no ordinary carpet. If you sit on it, it will take you through the air wherever you wish..."

What a present that would make, thought the prince, and he said aloud, "As it costs so much I must try it out first."

And so he sat down upon the carpet with the old man behind him, and he ordered the carpet to take them round the town and back again. What an amazing journey it was too! Husein's head was still spinning long after they came back to earth!

Now he did not hesitate. He paid up to the very last gold coin, and then, as there were many months before the end of the year when he was to meet his brothers, he sat on the carpet again, deciding to visit distant lands...

Prince Ali chose the path to the left, and it led him into green hills which

250

rolled down under high mountain peaks capped with snow. He journeyed
for four months till he came to the city of Shiraz in distant Persia.

The moment he saw the sumptuous markets, the workshops and the
palaces, which were richer far than those of Bishanghar, he knew he would
find here what he was searching for.

He was not disappointed, though for the first two days he wandered in
vain. But on the third day his attention was caught by shouts from the
market place. "A magic tube of ivory for sale, a magic tube!"

"How much do you want for that tube?" the prince asked the seller.

The man pulled him aside by the sleeve. "Thirty five thousand pieces of
gold," he whispered. "But it possesses a wondrous quality. When you look

into it, you will see whatever you wish, though it may be a thousand miles away..."

"Lend it to me, so I can see for myself," Ali asked, thinking of his father. And sure enough, the moment he put his eye near the glass lens set in the ivory, he saw the Indian king on the familiar gold throne.

"I shall be glad to buy it," said the prince, taking the tube from his eye. And he paid the man there and then.

"Who could bring a more valuable gift than I?" he said to himself, as he wandered away from the market. There was ample time before he had to return home, so he spent another four months in the lovely land of Persia.

The youngest prince Ahmed was left to take the middle road. For six long months he travelled, through deserts and forests, plains and mountains, till he stopped at last in the city of Samarkand — the furthest point from where he bade his brothers goodbye.

Like Husein and Ali, Ahmed too was fortunate. The city was so magnificent that he gasped with admiration, and a gift for his cousin was there, as if waiting for him. Before he even got off his horse, a young boy ran to him, a lovely apple in his hand.

"Buy this apple, sir, for it is no ordinary fruit..."

"How much do you want for it?" asked the prince, whose throat was dry after the long journey, and he was tempted by the fruit.

"This is not just a common apple," the boy continued, his face serious. "It contains medicine for all illnesses, and it will even cure a dying man, if he only smells it. Give me forty thousand gold pieces, and it is yours."

"Not so fast, young lad," Ahmed laughed, but his heart missed a beat with excitement. What a present this would make for his cousin! "I must convince myself first!" And he went in search of a man who was desperately ill.

He enquired in the streets, and eventually came to a house where a very old man, thin and withered, was preparing for death to take him. The prince hastened to his bedside and asked him to sniff the apple. Wonder of wonders! Before his eyes the yellow face of the dying man turned a healthy pink, his eyes cleared and he sat up in bed without any difficulty and shouted to his servant to bring food at once, for he was remarkably hungry.

That was enough for Ahmed. He counted out the forty thousand pieces of gold, handed them over to the boy and hid the precious fruit in his saddle bag.

Turning his horse round, he set off on his return journey without wasting

any time. He had a very long way to travel. But, when after six months
he reached the crossroads, his brothers were already waiting.

He embraced them affectionately and asked impatiently what gifts they
were bringing to the princess. Meantime he himself was taking out the
apple from the saddle bag with the greatest care.

"I have brought a flying carpet," Husein said, and Ali told him excitedly,
"I am bringing a magic tube, which shows you whatever you want to
see..."

"Let us use it now!" Ahmed cried enthusiastically. "Let us see what our
cousin is doing at this very minute right now."

The second brother placed his eye against the tube and immediately his
face paled.

"Nur en Nahar is dying," he stuttered, hardly able to speak. "I see her
lying motionless on her bed, and everyone there is weeping."

"Even the magic carpet won't help us," sobbed Husein. But Ahmed cried, "Yes it will, for I have an apple which will cure her. Quickly get on the carpet, both of you..."

The brothers flew through the princess's window like a tornado, and before anyone round her had a chance to realize what was happening, Nur en Nahar was already sitting up in bed, rubbing her eyes as if she had wakened from a long sleep.

"Oh, I dreamed I was dying," she murmured, looking perplexed. "It was no dream," Ahmed told her. "My magic apple saved you."

Now that the danger of death was over, the princes started to relate all that had happened during their travels, and spoke of the rare gifts they had brought. Then they waited with some impatience for their father to choose the one who was to be Nur en Nahar's husband.

But the king scratched his bearded chin thoughtfully and said. "There is no doubt that Ahmed's apple has saved the princess's life. But were it not for the magic tube and the flying carpet, it would have been useless. The three gifts are equally rare and wonderous, therefore it is necessary for you to compete further. The one who with his bow will shoot an arrow the furthest will be the winner!"

The very next day the princes decided to hold the shooting competition. They selected for their purpose a meadow, which stretched from the palace as far as the distant mountains.

Husein the eldest was the first to try. He aimed, and the arrow sped through the air, flying so far that all the court murmured in admiration.

Ali was the next to shoot. His arrow travelled even further, and the spectators' astonishment rewarded his effort.

The youngest prince was not downhearted by the success of his brothers. His arrow flew from his bow with such speed that no one even saw it.

Nor could anyone find it —there was not a trace of it anywhere. But the king had decided. "Ali, my second son is the one who deserves the princess, and he will have her as his wife. His arrow travelled further than Husein's, and it is unthinkable that Ahmed could have done better!"

The brothers accepted their father's judgement with meekness. But while the happy Ali prepared for the wedding, the sad Husein went away into the desert, there to live the life of a poor, pious dervish.

Ahmed could not get the thought of the lost arrow out of his head. He wandered towards the foothills of the mountains where the grassy meadow ended. When he reached them, exhausted and weary, he found his arrow wedged in a rocky cleft.

He took it out very carefully. He could not understand how the arrow had travelled so far — at least twice the distance of Ali's arrow.

Ahmed then noticed that the point of the arrow was missing. He searched around, till his gaze fell on a nearby dark cave. Suddenly it seemed the inner darkness was alight. Concealed iron gates were now opening and inside falling sunbeams shone upon a most beautiful maiden clothed in a grey blue robe woven from mists...

The astonished prince hardly dared to breathe. This surely must be a fairy, he thought, and as if in answer the voice of this lovely creature spoke. "I am the fairy Pari Banu, Prince Ahmed. It was I who commanded the wind to bring your arrow all the way here, and who broke off its point. Here it is."

She opened her hand, and on her palm lay a fragment of shining metal. Then she continued. "I have loved you for a very long time now, and I should so much like you to be my husband. That is why I led you into these mountains. Tell me whether you share my wish..."

The prince was speechless, incapable of uttering a single word. Why, Pari Banu's unearthly beauty was a thousand times greater than that of his cousin Nur en Nahar!

"How could I fail to share your wish," he managed to stammer at last. "But who is to give permission for our marriage? After all, I must first write out the wedding agreement with your father, as is customary!"

"Our laws are different from those of your people," the fairy said with a smile. "In this kingdom I am the queen, and I myself decide all matters. You are my husband from this moment."

As soon as she had pronounced these words, the iron gates closed with a clash behind them, and Pari Banu led Ahmed into her homeland. He felt as if he had stepped straight into a fairy tale. In large, beautiful gardens filled with flowering, scented roses, hibiscus plants, oleander and tamarisk stood crystal palaces, and before them lovely damsels of breathtaking beauty sang and danced on velvety green lawns.

"The wedding celebrations will now begin," said the fairy queen. "It is time for us to join in them."

Pari Banu's palace was more magnificent than any of the others. Behind glass walls, under arched gold ceilings, tables had already been prepared, lavishly laden with the most delicious dishes and bottles of the rarest wines. Haunting music trembled softly in the air like the breath of a spring breeze...

The wedding of prince Ahmed and the fairy queen lasted for one hundred days and one hundred nights, and with each passing day the prince loved his wife more dearly.

He did not give his father or brothers thought till half a year had passed — and then it flew like a small cloud across his clear brow. What were his father and his brothers doing? They surely must think that by now he had perished. He must visit them and dispel their fears.

He thought about this for several days, till Pari Banu herself spoke, "I know you are unhappy, my prince, and I shall gladly permit you to visit your father. But you are not to reveal to anyone where you live, nor who is your wife. I fear that if you do not heed my warning our happiness will be shortlived."

Ahmed gladly assured his wife that their life would remain their secret; he knew she was blessed with much wisdom and foresight.

Pari Banu gathered together many valuable gifts for the Indian king. She chose thirty riders to accompany Ahmed, and then bade him farewell by the iron gates of the cave.

"When you return here, have no fear. No ordinary mortal will see these gates — but to you they will open of their own accord."

What had been happening in the meantime at the court of the Indian king?

When Ahmed had disappeared so mysteriously, his father ordered an extensive search, but it brought no results. It was then that the grand vizier recommended an artful witch as the king's advisor. With the aid of magic she discovered that his youngest son was alive. The king rewarded her handsomely, and ever since then had sought her advice.

When Ahmed appeared he wept with happiness. It had been so long since his beloved son's disappearance. He listened to his tale, how well he was faring and how happy. He himself told him that Ali was now reigning in a distant part of the Indian empire, and that Husein still chose to live in a desolate land, but that he had become the most renowned of the dervishes. He did not press Ahmed to tell him his secret, so after three days the prince was able to return without fear of hindrance to Pari Banu.

It became his habit to visit his father every month. Each time he brought valuable gifts, each time he was accompanied by his grand bodyguard of thirty riders. Ahmed's father showed no curiosity but the witch and the vizier started evil whisperings into the king's ears. "Why doesn't Ahmed wish you to know where he now lives? He is up to no good, of that we are sure. He is only trying to blind you with his gifts. The place he comes from surely cannot be far distant, for the horses are never tired or sweaty. We warn you, do not trust him, or you will regret it. Soon he will want to oust you from your throne. Mark our words and Allah be with you!"

They talked and talked in this way about the prince, till they succeeded in poisoning the king's mind and he began to listen to their words. He insisted that Ahmed tell him his secret. But his son kept the promise he had given to his fairy wife.

One day when Ahmed left the palace as usual, the witch decided to follow him from afar. But long before she came to the cave, the prince and his retinue had disappeared. In vain she searched for a path they could have taken. All she could see were bare rocks. The iron gates remained invisible to her, thanks to Pari Banu's foresight.

The enraged witch strode up and down in a fury. Then she cried. "It doesn't matter; you may have outwitted me this time, but I'll be here waiting for you in a month's time."

She carried out her threat. When, after a month, the prince and his riders were leaving the cave, they saw an old woman lying on the path writhing in pain.

"Oh, my good people, please help me," she moaned. "I am dying!"

There was no other living soul about, so Prince Ahmed turned back towards the cave, and the iron gates reopened. The sorceress pretended that she had fainted with the pain, but she was keeping an eye on all that was taking place.

Pari Banu was standing where he had left her.

"Why have you returned, my prince?"

"We found this old woman nearby," Ahmed explained, pointing to her. "She is dying and is in agony."

"We will cure her," the queen decided and straightaway she ordered two maidens to take her into the palace. Next she brought out a golden dish.

"The water from the Lion spring is sure to make her well," she said, and wetting her fingers in the bowl, she rubbed them gently across the old woman's brow.

The witch opened her eyes as if by a miracle.

"You have saved my life, and God is sure to reward you. Who are you, My Lady?" she asked then.

"I am Pari Banu," the queen of the fairies replied. "But you must ask no further questions and go home now."

Though the old woman was besides herself with curiosity, she could do nothing but obey. The moment the iron gates closed behind her, she hurried to the palace, so that she would reach the Indian king before Prince Ahmed.

She told him what had happened and everything she had found out, adding, "Your son is far more powerful than you, My King, and Pari Banu could easily destroy you by raising her little finger. Put them to the test. Ask for some exceptional gift — then you will know whether they are well disposed towards you."

The king followed her advice as usual. He reproached the prince for keeping Pari Banu a secret for so long, then added slyly, "Your wife must have great powers and I am sure she will be glad to do me a small service. I need a tent large enough to take the whole of my army. When we are on manoeuvres, we cannot take along a tent for every member of the cavalry. I want one which can be loaded onto a single horse, but which will grow on demand to such a size that it will take the whole army."

With a heavy heart, the prince delivered his father's request to the fairy queen. But Pari Banu said, "My beloved husband, your father's wish is easily granted. Look here." And she showed him the palm of her hand. On it sat a tiny brightly coloured tent.

"When it is placed on the ground, it grows to a size large enough to hold the entire Indian army and their weapons. I shall gladly send it to your father."

After a month had elapsed, Prince Ahmed visited his father as was his custom, taking with him the magic tent. But in the meantime the sorceress had been at work again, and had persuaded the king to demand another gift the following month — this time the magic water from the Lion Spring. Then, she said, they would be quite sure of his son's true feelings.

On this occasion the task was not easy even for Pari Banu. For the magic water came from the courtyard of a mountain castle, and this castle was guarded by four lions. Only the wit and wisdom of the fairy queen prevented them from tearing Ahmed apart when he rode among them. Following her advice he threw them four enormous chunks of meat, and the moment he had filled his jug from the spring, he galloped off like the wind.

"Now I know your father means to kill you," said the fairy upon his return. "You must take the greatest care when you are in his palace."

By that time the witch had succeeded in making the king believe that

Ahmed longed to sit on his throne and thought of nothing else. Now both the witch and the king wondered how to be rid of him for good.

"If he does not bring the water from the Lion Spring, he will die in prison," the king declared. But the sorceress objected, "He will assuredly bring it, just to quieten your suspicions. I have a better idea. There is a certain dwarf living in this world who kills everyone he meets with his steel cudgel. He is only three feet tall, but his beard sticks out thirty feet in front of him. I do not know of a single person who has met him and lived. Order your son to bring this dwarf here. By his hand Ahmed will die without blame being attached to yourself." The witch laughed wickedly.

How astonished the king was when he received the water from the Lion Spring! He thanked his son and entertained him royally for the rest of his stay. But when they bade each other goodbye, the King said, "The tasks I have set you have carried out to my satisfaction. I have only one more wish. Bring me the dwarf with the long beard. They say he is only three feet

high, and that he carries a steel cudgel on his shoulder. I am sure this desire you fulfill without difficulty and I promise I shall ask from you nothing more."

What was the prince to do?

He hurried back to his crystal palace and told Pari Banu of his father's latest whim.

"This is what I feared," the fairy cried. "The dwarf does exist and is called Daibar. But the king did not tell you that he uses his steel cudgel to kill anyone who comes near. Your father knows that through Daibar he will be rid of you."

"I refuse to satisfy my father's desire. I never wish to lay my eyes on him again," the prince said decisively.

"Have no fear, no harm will come to you," the fairy queen spoke softly. "Daibar is my blood brother. Our enemies are not aware of that. So it will be enough for me to ask him to do you no harm and to go with you to your father's palace."

They did not speak of the matter again.

A month later, however, the dwarf was waiting for Ahmed in front of the cave. He truly was a most horrific creature. The long, fiery red beard was as hard and as sharp as steel needles; his eyes were lost in his swollen cheeks and his nose drooped towards his chin. He swung his cudgel over his head with frightening speed and such dexterity that it whistled as it whirled through the air. But he welcomed the prince quite kindly.

"I am happy to know you and I shall gladly help you. But if you were not the husband of my blood sister Pari Banu, you would have not fared so well. I mean to destroy the whole human race with my cudgel," he added threateningly.

For Ahmed the journey to the palace passed like a dream. The moment the dwarf approached the gates, the guards scattered in fright. The same thing happened in the forecourt. Whoever could took to their heels — the emirs, the soldiers, the servants. And all Daibar did was toss his cudgel round his head and smile merrily.

They entered the palace. The prince could not help laughing at the panic and commotion which then followed. Everyone disappeared as if someone had waved a magic wand — everyone but the king, his vizier and the witch. They were rooted to the spot in sheer terror.

"Why did you call me to you?" asked Daibar, approaching the throne threateningly. The terrified king did not utter a word. "So you would make

262

a fool of me, would you?" stormed the dwarf, and swinging his cudgel, he killed with one swift blow the king, the sly vizier and the wicked witch.

"Now you will reign in India!" he cried, turning to the prince. And Daibar set the prince on the throne. His eyes wandered for a moment round the hall, then he slung his cudgel over his shoulder and went away, humming happily. "Give greetings and love to my sister Pari Banu!" he shouted as he left.

As soon as the dwarf disappeared, the royal palace sprang to life again. The servants, the soldiers, the guards, the emirs and judges gathered round and all of them proclaimed glory to their king, Ahmed and their queen, Pari Banu, begging them humbly to rule wisely and justly to the end of their days.